BENEATH
STILL
WATERS

a novel by

CYNTHIA A. GRAHAM

Blank Slate Press | Saint Louis, MO

Blank Slate Press
Saint Louis, MO 63110

For information, contact
Blank Slate Press at 3963 Flora Place, Saint Louis, MO 63110.
www.blankslatepress.com

Blank Slate Press is an imprint of Amphora Publishing Group LLC.

Manufactured in the United States of America
Cover Design by Kristina Blank Makansi
Cover Art: Shutterstock

Library of Congress Control Number: 2015934030
ISBN: 9780991305841

For my father, Lloyd Greenfield, who believed in magic.

BENEATH STILL WATERS

I

Hick Blackburn pulled his hat over his eyes and squinted against the silver sun flickering and blinking on the surface of the slough's black water. Mosquitoes and gnats buzzed around the brush that lined the shore as frogs began their night choruses. The trees, heavy with summer leafing, were suffocating in their density, and his chest felt tight and heavy, the closeness pressing in on him. He surveyed the murky pond once more, and then turned his attention back to Billy Ponder.

"You say it was caught in the brush?" he asked.

Billy nodded. His clothes hung damp from his skinny frame. He scratched a mosquito bite with his foot and told Hick, "Jimmy and me was commencing to string the wire across the slough, to keep the hogs from wandering off. We started on the other side and had just passed from the deep part to the western edge when he stepped on something."

"And it was the infant?"

Billy's face grew visibly pale. He licked his lips and his

eyes darted to Jimmy Scott, inconsolable in the back of a pickup truck. "Yeah," he answered. "It was the baby."

"You say it was on this end of the slough?"

"Yes sir," the boy answered. He cracked his knuckles and there was a tremor in his voice. "The water's so dark you can't see the bottom. He didn't know what it was 'til he brought it up." Here his voice faltered and he shifted his glance, again, to his friend.

The young boy in the truck bed sobbed, distracting Hick for a moment. "What time was it?"

"Right around five o'clock. We been working all day and was just about done."

"And there were no clothes, nothing on the baby that could identify where it might have come from?"

Billy shook his head. "No, sir. She was naked when he pulled her out of the water. Then he screamed and dropped it. At first, I thought it was a snappin' turtle got him the way he was blubbering and carrying on. Then I seen her floating there and we got out of the water fast and ran to Jimmy's house. His daddy pulled the baby out and then went and got Deputy Kinion."

Hick wrote this information on a pad of paper. *Jesus*, he thought, *Roy Michaels was sheriff for forty years and never dealt with anything like this*. Dusk began to smudge away the daylight, and he pushed his hat back and ran his hand across his eyes. Reading his notes over again, he decided the boy could offer no more help. He closed the barely used leather book with a snap.

"Who do you think she is?" Billy asked in a small voice.

Hick scanned the water, trying to make sense of where the child might have come from, but something in the boy's voice made him pause. The magnitude of the day's events washed over him. What a gruesome discovery for two fourteen-year-olds. Awkwardly, he patted Billy's shoulder. "Unfortunately, we may never know. You guys gonna be okay?"

Billy managed an unconvincing, "Yeah."

Cherokee Crossing's doctor, Jake Prescott, made his way over to the edge of the slough, trudging through the thick, muddy grass. A short, heavy man, the heat did not agree with him. He paused to wipe the sweat from his neck with a handkerchief and removed a fat unlit cigar from his mouth. "Damned mess is what it is," he grumbled as he and Hick walked toward the tent Adam and Wash, Hick's deputies, had set up near the slough. "Son of a bitch, Hick, how long you been sheriff?"

"A year this month."

Dr. Prescott stopped and looked up at him. "Been that long already?"

"Days like this make it seem even longer." At just twenty-two-years old, Andrew Jackson "Hick" Blackburn was the youngest sheriff ever elected in Cherokee Crossing, Arkansas. His name had been put on the ballot as a sort of joke, the other two deputies urging him on. But they had been deputies long enough that each had made enemies, and Hick was new, fresh with the novelty of just arriving home from World War II. It had been the closest election in years, and the outcome shocked the young man. Some days it still shocked him.

Wash Metcalf and Adam Kinion were waiting in the tent. Wash had been deputy since Hick was a boy, and both deputies had worked for Sheriff Michaels. They were seasoned veterans. Most things didn't bother them, but this wasn't like most things.

"I ain't never seen the like," Wash said. Hick had always known Wash and knew he and Sheriff Michaels had been good at their jobs. They had broken up hog stealing rings, closed down gambling joints, and confiscated moonshine stills, but in Cherokee Crossing, infants were buried, not tossed into the slough. Nothing like this had ever happened before. Wash took his handkerchief and ran it across his balding head with a trembling hand.

Bracing himself, Hick moved to the examining table. On it laid the remains of a baby girl, badly decomposed and headless. His stomach turned queasy as the heat enveloped him. It rushed to his head at once and he closed his eyes, fighting to get his emotions under control. He had fought in Europe and had seen plenty of death, but this brought back images he wasn't prepared to deal with. He rested his hand on the table to steady himself, and his eyes caught Jake's concerned expression.

"What can you tell me, Doc?" he asked with forced calmness.

The doctor pulled out a clipboard and proceeded. "It is a female, Caucasian, with the umbilical cord still attached. Mind you, it's very hard to make any kind of determination. The body is macerated; the skin is slipping."

"Exactly what is it you're trying to determine?"

Jake's eyes met Hick's over the clipboard. "There's a good chance this child was a live birth."

"Son of a bitch." Hick's mind raced with the implications. "Is there any way to tell how she died?"

"The good news is she was not decapitated."

That was a relief. For a brief moment, he thought they might be dealing with a maniac. "How do you know?"

"See up here, around the neck," the doctor said pointing his cigar at the place in question. Hick forced his eyes to follow the cigar, but his stomach flopped and he felt suffocated. He had never seen a headless body; it took all of his resolve to pay attention to the doctor. "That was not done with a knife or sharp object. It is rough and uneven. I believe the head was eaten off by turtles."

"The hell you say." Adam turned away in disgust, wiping his mouth roughly with the back of his hand.

"I do say," the doctor returned.

Hick glanced up at Adam. He had been deputy and his brother-in-law for a dozen years, and in all that time Hick could not recall Adam being shaken by anything. But, above all, Adam was a family man. It would be impossible for him to remain detached with four little boys of his own at home. Hick turned his attention back to the child on the table. "Is there any way to determine how long she's been here?"

"Can't really say for sure. The body bloats and decays more quickly in water. It could be anywhere from a week to a month."

"Anyone around town expecting during that time?"

"Plenty," the doctor answered. "Would you like me to

check on the ones I know … see how they're progressing?"

"That would be a help."

"Well, then," the doctor told him gathering his equipment and putting his light colored jacket back on. "I'll let you know."

"There'll be a coroner's inquest on this tomorrow," Hick said. "I know it's a good drive to the county seat and it's short notice, but they ain't gonna want to wait with this one. Is that okay with you?"

Jake's eyes went back to the child. "I'll be there … just say when."

The doctor turned to leave, with Adam and Wash close behind. Hick lingered behind in the tent and glanced back at the child. Impetuously, he touched the tiny hand. It was clenched in a fist, cold and perfect. He felt his eyes smart, and blinked, quickly looking away.

"He's here again," Wash called into the tent.

Hick looked up. "Murphy?"

Wash nodded.

Wayne Murphy, the town's newspaperman, was a meddlesome pest. "Great. Every detail will be splattered all over the paper tomorrow. I want him the hell out of here. You tell him it's a possible crime scene and he don't need to be poking around."

Wash left and Hick covered the child with the sheet. He stepped out of the tent and joined the doctor in the chilly twilight that was descending on the slough. Dan Scott, Billy's father, spoke with Adam as Billy climbed up to join Jimmy in the back of the pickup truck. Hick watched as the men shook hands, and then Dan drove off with the two boys staring out at the slough.

"Poor bastards," Hick said shaking his head.

"It must have been a terrible shock," the doctor agreed. "A damned shame about the child … and so senseless, too."

"Let's not jump to any conclusions," Hick cautioned. "I'll send the baby to your office for the autopsy."

The doctor nodded, but added, "But if it was murder … why?"

"Why indeed?" thought Hick as he drove home later that evening. Faint moonlight showed through the clouds, barely illuminating the rows and rows of cotton on each side of the dirt road. His nostrils flared as he sucked in the sweet smell of turned earth and impending rain wafting in through the open windows.

He took his hat off, set it on the seat beside him, and ran his fingers through his hair. Why kill a baby? Perhaps it was just a stillborn that someone had buried on their own property and dogs had dug up. Certainly they should have notified him, but that wasn't a crime. Maybe they didn't even know. But one thing nagged at him. He hadn't heard of anyone losing a baby, especially one near full term … it was a small town and things like that did not remain quiet. It appeared the slough was a secret grave, an intentional hiding place of some closely guarded shame.

He stretched and undid his tie, unbuttoning the top button. It had been a long day and promised to be a long investigation, if the coroner deemed a crime had taken place. Such a tiny child to cause such a huge commotion.

He found a cigarette and lit it. He only smoked when alone and troubled, and tonight he was both. Inhaling deeply, he let the smoke curl out slowly from the corner of his mouth while he kept his eyes fixed on the headlight beams illuminating the dusty road before him. The grinding of gravel under tires was as monotonous as the scenery, but the occasional loud *clink* and *thunk* of a rock flipped against the car kept his mind from wandering too far.

A familiar sense of uncertainty swelled around him, and he shook his head and tossed the cigarette out the window. The rawness was unwelcome. The moments of self-doubt coming more often and darker, blacker than before. When he was younger, there was nothing he couldn't do. That was before Belgium, before the marches in the rain with hundred pound packs, before the discovery of the dark farmhouse….

He forced himself to put those thoughts aside. It does no good to dwell on the past, he told himself yet again. Besides, maybe the coroner would declare the death to be by natural causes and put the whole thing to rest. He put his hat back on, pulling it far over his eyes, knowing full well this was not a case he had the ability to solve. To find the killer of a child, a nameless, faceless infant … that would be impossible.

2

Squatting on his haunches, with his hands hanging languidly between his legs, Hick stared at the smooth, dark water of Jenny Slough. It was near dawn and a thin mist of vapor rose from the surface of the water into the cool morning air. He looked relaxed as he squatted, like a fisherman contemplating the day's opportunities. But a close observer would know this was not the case.

His eyes darted across the water, observant and alert. With meticulous care, he studied every square inch of dirt around the slough, trying to find any clue as to who might have stepped there. In the war he had learned a perfect stillness, a way to conduct himself without moving any part of his body, save his eyes. A false movement in battle could cost a man his life, and this stillness, this detachment, even from himself, had become habit. Years of being a soldier had ingrained lessons that could never be unlearned.

Few people lived in the vicinity of the swamp and none at this end. The houses on the other end of the slough, those belonging to the Thompsons, the Scotts, and the Pringles, were too far from this point to offer much help. Witnesses would probably not be an option.

The dim gray of the breaking dawn was moist and sticky, as its chill stuck to his skin, uncomfortable and damp. Though his muscles ached, he didn't acknowledge them, instead waiting, watching, letting the sounds of the waking world surround him. Hick had grown to love the night, the nocturnal hush helping to ease his troubled soul. He'd been waiting for two hours, hoping first light would reveal some clue, elucidate something unseen. *Might as well wait here as at home.* Another sleepless night had caused his head to ache and his stomach to turn. The nightmares were easy compared with this utter lack of sleep.

When his eyes closed, he was haunted by the image of the infant, sprawled on the table, headless, reminding him of the hens his mother would roast. It was one thing to kill a man in battle with his gun aimed at your head. But this killing of innocence, *this* was another thing altogether. He shuddered at a sudden unwelcome vision, one he had squelched since arriving home from the front.

"I thought I might find you here."

Hick turned to see Jake Prescott making his way toward him. The doctor looked weary and troubled.

"Morning, Doc," Hick said in a tired voice. "You're up early."

The doctor pulled a cigar out of his shirt pocket and lit it. "Had trouble sleeping. You?"

"Same," Hick replied, rising and lighting a cigarette. The

two men stood silently for a moment, smoke hanging in the air around them.

"It's strange how some places on earth never seem to change," Jake said after a while. "I can remember coming out here to fish with your daddy when we were boys. It was exactly the same as it is now." Hick was wearing the flannel shirt he always wore to fish in, the one that had been his father's. "You could be him standing here in that shirt."

Hick's face darkened a little. "I could never be him." He paused and took a drag from his cigarette. "You're forgetting, he was the 'magic man'." He forced a thin smile.

"Nonsense. Superstitious nonsense," the doctor barked. "Your father hated that distinction. He was above it."

A small laugh escaped Hick. "He did hate it. The seventh son of a seventh son. People would bang on our doors at all hours thinking he could heal them. I remember women asking him to breathe in their baby's mouths for the thrush. It was embarrassing." After a pause, he added, "Didn't do him much good in the end, anyway, now did it?"

The doctor took the chewed cigar from his mouth. "No, it didn't. No one lives forever, not even seventh sons of seventh sons."

It was a bitter pill for Hick to swallow...the first letter he received from home after arriving on the frozen battlefield. He was eighteen, alone in his tent, tears frozen on his face. He left the letter behind, crumpled and squashed into the snow.

"Hick, I have to recommend an investigation into the infant's death. I think it was a homicide."

Hick closed his eyes. He wasn't surprised, but he'd hoped it wasn't the case. "Why?"

"Because I believe the child was perfectly healthy when it was born. The autopsy showed froth and sand in the airway, hypostasis around the heart muscle, the lungs were inflated and heavy with water. She even had sand in her stomach. There is too much evidence here to not do some sort of investigation."

Hick took a long drag from his cigarette. The sun was beginning to change the feel of the air, the comforting peace of darkness replaced with the harsh light of day. Without looking at the doctor, he asked, "I just wonder what good will come from an investigation."

Jake Prescott turned to him with a confused expression. "What do you mean?"

"I mean if there is someone out there who didn't want the child … some woman who was in a bind … what good will come out of locking her up?"

The doctor said nothing and Hick took advantage of the pause. "Let's say it was one of the girls at the high school. Do you really want to see her brought up on murder charges? Or some poor farmer's wife? I just wonder … is this really something we want to do?"

The bright red end of the doctor's cigar stood out against the dusty morning light. Puffing thoughtfully, he finally said, "I understand your point, Hick. Let me ponder it. You gotta understand, though, I don't tell you how to do your job and I don't expect you to tell me how to do mine. I'll consider what you said, but I want you to consider something. A life was taken here at this slough. Granted, she was a person nobody knew, there is no one mourning her, no one missing her. That doesn't take away from the fact that a violent act occurred right where we're standing. This could be infanticide. I see your point … you must see mine."

Hick removed his hat, ran his fingers through his short light hair. He put it back on, tilted down over his eyes. The war had taken a toll. Old notions of right and wrong had been confused, shattered by the cold reality that some seemed to lay more claims to life than others. He took another drag and watched the smoke. It was fleeting, evaporating into nothingness. "I hear your point, Doc, but I also believe this person is no threat to the community. I don't see it happening again. What would be the harm if we just let the dead rest in peace?"

"And it doesn't bother you?" the doctor asked. "The fact that someone could live and die and simply be forgotten?"

Shivering in the morning's chill, Hick answered, "It happens. There are holes all over Europe filled with the remains of people who will never be remembered. People who suffered more than that baby girl. I ain't saying it's right. I'm just saying it might be better to let things lie."

Jake smiled a little. "You remember when the Hughes boys lit that cat on fire. It took your daddy all day to get you to stop crying. He told me later it was your mother's doing. Always said you took everything to heart because your mother protected and babied you after your brother died." He turned and looked into Hick's face. "Life was never held cheap in your house, Hick. Never."

"I'm not saying life is cheap," he countered, turning away. "Sometimes it's just more quickly spent."

The doctor paused and then said, "I'll think about what you said. I best get home and get ready for the inquest."

Hick glanced down at his flannel shirt. He rarely left home without his sheriff's uniform on. It was, without fail, meticulously pressed, the tie perfect, never a button missing, his shoes bright and polished, his face clean shaven, his hair neat.

Turning to leave, Jake paused. "By the way, Murphy's printed another unflattering story about you in the paper."

"About the infant?"

The doctor nodded.

"How'd he find out?"

"The boys."

"Damn. Why does he hate me?"

"If it weren't you, it'd be someone else. He likes to drum up controversy."

"What's he say?"

"What you'd expect. That with our inept law enforcement, we'll probably never know how some poor child ended up in the slough. Of course, it's his job to get everyone all riled up. Helps sell papers."

Taking one last drag, Hick threw his cigarette into the water. "He's probably right anyway. It would sure make my life easier if the coroner declared the death to be by natural causes. It's entirely possible the child was dug up from a shallow grave. Dogs could have done it, or coyotes, maybe even a panther."

"Maybe. I suppose anything's possible." Jake eyed him intently. "But do you really think that's what happened here?"

Hick crossed his arms over his chest, staring out over the water. He didn't know that his shoulders were slumped, that his thin frame seemed bent with anxiety. Finally, after a pause, he blurted, "Doc, this is impossible. We've got nothing on this baby … not even her hair or eye color."

"I'm sorry you're put into such a position."

"You know, almost two out of every three people in this town didn't want me to be sheriff. I think about that every day. If I had thought for a second I might win, my name would have never been on that ballot."

"You're doing fine."

Hick shook his head. "Mule and Hoyt Smith got away with busting into the post office because I screwed up the investigation. If I had only waited for Adam or Wash to get there, they wouldn't have."

"No one blames you."

Bitterly, Hick laughed. "Wayne Murphy blames me."

"Wayne Murphy would blame Jesus Christ himself if it would sell papers. Wayne has one god and one god only, and that's the dollar bill. The truth ain't so important to him as long as he can stir the pot and get everyone worked up about something. Hick, you didn't do nothing wrong at that post office. It wouldn't have mattered who got there first. Just so happened it was you that got the blame."

Looking at his feet, Hick absentmindedly noted his shoes could use some polish. He felt inadequate, inadequate for everything. "Doc, do you ever feel like you just can't do it? Like you've been given a task and it's just too big for you?"

"All the time," the doctor replied.

"And what do you do?"

"I do my best. Sometimes I fail. I failed with your daddy, I failed with others. I at least have the satisfaction of knowing I did everything I could."

Hick's eyes turned up. His face had a boyish quality, round wide eyes and open eyebrows, a wide nose and pointed chin. He looked like a schoolboy searching for the right answer to his teacher's question.

Jake gave him a small, encouraging smile and then threw his cigar down on the sandy bank, grinding it out with his shoe. "I'll see you this afternoon. We can ride together to the county seat. I'll consider what you said before I make my recommendation, but I'm not promising anything."

"Thanks," Hick called after him as the sun broke the tree line and lit up the slough.

3

"Hickory, you look awful," Magdalene Benson said as she poured him a cup of coffee at the diner that morning. Maggie was the only one who still called him Hickory, testament to an ancient intimacy.

He took a gulp and swallowed. "Just didn't sleep well, that's all." Black circles ringed his eyes and his haggard appearance betrayed more than one restless night.

Placing the pot onto the warmer, she returned to the counter and lingered in front of him in spite of the Saturday morning rush. "Want to talk about it?"

What was there to talk about? The coroner's inquest was just hours away and he felt cornered by Jake Prescott. "It's just the infant," he told her, lowering his voice. "I hoped we were all on the same page about this … that it was probably a stillborn. But I saw Doc this morning and he seems pretty convinced it was a homicide."

The blood drained from Maggie's face. "A homicide?" she whispered. "Someone murdered the child?"

Hick shrugged his shoulders and turned his eyes down toward his coffee cup.

"Who would have done something like that?" she asked. He glanced up and her face was pale.

"Could be the child was illegitimate and put into the slough by its mother."

"Her own mother?"

Hick gulped his coffee. "There's only so much the law can do. Personally, I'm ready to let the whole thing go and let the child rest in peace. No amount of detective work is going to bring her back." He glanced up and saw her eyes harden, the familiar stark line of disapproval formed between her eyebrows. He shook his head. "Oh, great, not you, too."

"I don't know what you're talking about."

"Don't give me that, Mag, I know that look. Listen, what good is it going to do to track this woman down and lock her up? What's that going to solve?"

"A murder, for one thing."

"You and the doc."

"Well?"

His hat lay on the counter beside the coffee cup and he picked at the lint. "I don't think I can do it. I don't think I can find the person who did this." He focused angry eyes on her. "Are you satisfied? Is that what you wanted to hear?"

"Don't be stupid."

"Well, God almighty, I don't know what everyone wants from me. Let's say the baby was killed. It could be anyone in this town, or the next. The mother could be a gypsy or an itinerant worker. The only thing I can tell you, is the baby was white and female. That's it. Period." He put his elbow on the counter and covered his eyes. He hated this feeling of helplessness.

Maggie leaned over the counter, and without thinking, began stroking his arm with her fingertips. "Hickory, no one expects a miracle. But you are at least going to try, aren't you?"

Her touch was comforting, and, like always, flooded him with memories—their first date, their first dance, their first kiss—and he felt himself wanting to respond. He wanted to squeeze the hand that caressed him, twine his fingers with hers, but instead, he withdrew. She straightened up and stepped backward.

Defensively, she pulled the pad out of her apron and suddenly seemed very far away. "What do you want for breakfast today?"

He couldn't let himself look at her. "Just coffee," he mumbled. And then she was gone.

After finishing another cup, he crossed the street and paused in front of the station. Each day he glanced at the sign hanging on the door that read "Sheriff A. J. Blackburn." His friends had started calling him Hickory in grammar school when they learned that was Andrew Jackson's nickname. It had been shortened in high school and now everyone but his mother and Magdalene called him Hick. A. J. Blackburn seemed like somebody else.

Adam sat with his feet propped up on his desk.

"Late night?" he asked. Adam had married Hick's sister twelve years earlier, on Pam Blackburn's eighteenth birthday. He was eighteen years older than Hick's sister and had taken the role of older brother to Hick. Today, however, Hick wasn't in the mood for any homespun advice.

"Late and lonely."

Adam shook his head laughing. "Boy, you got to get out more." Hick hated to be called "boy." His hair still had cowlicks in it, his skin was smooth, and at times, blemished, but his eyes were stormy and tired.

"Where'd you eat breakfast?" Adam asked him.

"Diner."

Adam sat forward in his chair and looked at Hick with a knowing expression. "She ain't gonna wait forever."

Hick looked away. There were times he genuinely hated living in a small town, where everything was known to everyone. This was not a conversation he was in the mood to have. He tried to go to his desk, but Adam put his legs on the trash can blocking his way.

"What's eating you, boy?"

"Do you really have to ask? The baby we found in the slough. How in hell do you suppose we're gonna find out who killed it? You got any ideas, 'cause I'm open. I've got nothing."

"Doc didn't come up with anyone?"

"Not yet."

Adam laughed. "Well, that would have made it just a little too easy, don't you think?"

Hick envied Adam. With his easy manner and self-confidence he would have made the perfect sheriff. He had grown up in Cherokee Crossing, married, had children, was an upstanding citizen.

Hick hung his hat on the coat rack and sat down at his desk, putting his head in his hands.

"I thought we had come to the conclusion it was a still-born and decided not to pursue it."

"We did," Hick agreed. "Apparently, Doc has different ideas. I saw him earlier and he started babbling about murder and infanticide. I know what he's going to tell the coroner, and I can pretty much guess what the coroner will rule."

"If they rule it a homicide, we investigate it as such," Adam calmly reasoned.

Hick shook his head. "And how do you suppose we do that?"

"I'll go back up to the slough and have a look around," Adam replied rising from his desk and grabbing his hat. "Maybe there's some clue we missed."

"Thanks, Adam."

Adam paused at the doorway. "You know, there's only so much we can do. You've got nothing to prove."

Unlike Adam, Hick felt he had plenty to prove. He turned his chair to look out the window at the people of Cherokee Crossing as they conducted their daily business. He never revealed the insecurities inside, but he felt the lack of confidence in the townsfolk everywhere he went.

The door opened and he looked up to see Dr. Prescott. Inwardly, he groaned. "Hey," he said in a tired voice.

"Before we head over to the inquest, I've got something," the doctor told him.

"What do you mean?"

"It might be nothing, but it could be a clue. While I was doing the postmortem on the baby, I jotted down a few notes. There was a particular anomaly … a syndactylism of the third and fourth finger on the left hand."

Hick looked at him. "What?"

The doctor explained, "They were webbed. They were connected up above the first joint."

Hick scratched the inside of his ear and looked at the doctor with an eye closed. "I don't get it, Doc. How does that help me?"

"I've been reading up on syndactylism. Apparently, it can be genetic. It runs in families."

Hick's eyes lit with understanding. "You're telling me the baby's mama or daddy might have webbed fingers?"

The doctor shrugged. "At least it's something."

After a momentary silence, Hick leaned back in his chair and put his hands behind his head. "Tell me. Why is this so important to you?"

The doctor crossed the room and stood in front of Hick's desk. "Because the minute that child drew breath, she became the youngest citizen of this town. That entitles her to protection under the law."

Hick looked up at the ceiling and exhaled loudly, a feeling of resignation sweeping over him. "I reckon it does," he agreed.

He rose from his desk and reached for his hat. He paused, once more glancing out the window. The street was lined with cars, the sidewalk crowded with shoppers. This used to be Hick's world, a place he had known intimately before going into the army. Now, it seemed strange and foreign. He felt a continuous need to question what he saw, as if he couldn't trust his eyes or instincts. It no longer felt like home.

"Well, let's get this over with." They opened the door and went out into the June sunshine.

4

Dappled light shone through the leaves of the mimosa tree in Elsie Blackburn's front yard. Hick had learned at ten years of age it was a spindly tree when the branch he stood on bowed beneath him and he tumbled to the ground, breaking his arm. When they were children, Maggie picked the mimosa blossoms and put them in her hair, pretending they were feathers. The tree offered no wind break and little shade, but as he aged, Hick learned to appreciate it simply for its familiarity. It had been there, standing sentinel in his front yard, since before his birth.

"I'll be right out," Elsie called from inside. The top step cracked as Hick paused on it. He remembered with a tinge of guilt that he promised to replace it a month ago. His mother appeared at the door in her Sunday best, white gloves on each hand, a small hat sitting on top of her white hair. Age may have wrinkled her translucent skin, but it had done nothing to soften its rosiness or the brightness of the blue eyes that now looked at him worriedly. "Andrew, you look tired."

"Why do you still insist on calling me Andrew?" he asked opening the car door for her.

Her hand rested on his cheek and she smiled. "Because it's your name," she replied stubbornly.

Every Sunday since returning from the war, Hick took his mother to church. The old wooden Baptist Church had been part of his life as long as he could remember. Not as small and run down as the Pentecostal Church, or as large and pretentious as the brick Methodist church, the Second Baptist Church of Cherokee Crossing was a comfortable, middling place for the Blackburn family. He glanced next door at the Benson house. Maggie and her mother were already gone.

As he returned to his seat, he noticed his mother rummaging in her purse for her handkerchief. It was a nervous habit of hers; she always held a clenched handkerchief in her hand whenever she rode in a car. He started the engine and she asked, eying him closely, "Do you sleep well at night?"

He turned his head as they drove. "I sleep fine."

There was an uncomfortable pause. "I made a special dinner today," she said abruptly changing the subject. "Adam, Pam and the kids will be over."

"That's great. Diner food gets a little old."

"I'm sure the diner has other attractions," she replied with false innocence.

He glanced at her out of the sides of his eyes. "Oh, Ma. Don't start."

"Why don't you ask Maggie over for Sunday dinner? I would love to see her."

They pulled into the parking lot and Hick slammed the car door harder than he meant to. He moved around and opened his mother's door. "We'll see," was all he would say. That was the only way he could tell his mother no.

They climbed the concrete steps and entered the small sanctuary. Several men greeted Hick and his mother at the doorway. In Cherokee Crossing, church defined your life—those who attended were respected, and those who didn't were not. Hick mumbled pleasantries and shook hands all the while scanning the pews. Maggie, wearing a new summer dress, was sitting in her regular place with her mother.

"Come along, Andrew," his mother said grabbing his sleeve and leading him up the aisle. He found himself seated directly across from Maggie, and the sidelong glances his mother cast at him indicated it was not by accident.

Hick heard little of the sermon. His Bible was open, but his eyes were on Maggie's arms, the skin smooth, the line of muscle and bone, graceful. They were thin, elegant, even the shape of her hands was beautiful, the fingers long and exquisite. He remembered when they were children, the first time those fingertips brushed against his mouth as she shared her grapes with him. He had snatched her hand and kissed the fingers, and he would never forget the amused smile that played upon her dark lips.

Olive skin and deep brown eyes reflected the Cherokee blood that flowed through much of the population of that part of Arkansas. Maggie wasn't beautiful in the traditional sense of the word, instead she reminded him of a deer, slender and brown. Natural. Elemental.

The heat in the church was oppressive. The stuffy room offered no breeze, and the women around him pulled out their little fans. The swooshing noise was hypnotic and suddenly, he felt tired. The sleepless nights seemed to be catching up all at once, waiting for a time when he was forced to sit still so they could pounce on him. He blinked hard and held his eyes open as wide as they would go. The next thing he knew, everyone around him stood up to sing. He quickly rose, hoping no one had noticed. Glancing at Maggie, he saw her smile. Unhappily, he felt his face blush, a propensity he could never quite control.

When everyone began to file out into the hot June sunshine, Hick felt his mother's elbow poke into his back. "Ask her," she whispered.

"Ma—"

"Do it."

He crossed the aisle to where Maggie stood. "Mag?"

She turned and gave him a teasing smile. "I noticed today's sermon was not very interesting to you."

He shrugged. "It wasn't the sermon. I'm just a little tired."

She cocked her head to the side. "You feelin' okay?"

She looked concerned and it made him uncomfortable. Quickly changing the subject he said, "Listen, my mama made a big Sunday dinner and wanted to know if you'd like to join us."

"Your mama wants me to come to dinner?"

"Yeah."

"What about you?"

He was confused. "What do you mean? Of course you should come if you want to."

She shook her head. "That's not what I asked. Do *you* want me to come?"

He looked down into her face. What was wrong with him? Of course he wanted her to come over. He wanted her all the time, and yet he could never make himself tell her. It was as if there was a gag in his mouth, something that kept him from saying what he felt. There was no use in trying to speak, he had tried for over a year, and the words just wouldn't come. He was full of feelings, vast and mysterious that he was impotent to articulate. Inside he felt he was screaming, that surely she would hear him and know the truth, but he was helpless, silent. She looked at him, searching for the answer she wanted to hear. But he said nothing. Finally, her face changed, her eyes filling with such sadness that his heart began to ache.

"Just stop, Hickory ... please. I can't play this game with you forever. I don't know what you want from me, but I know what I want from life. I deserve another chance to live. You, at least, owe me that. If your mama wants to see me, I'll come another day." She turned and left and he stood unmoving in the aisle as all of the churchgoers filed out. Finally, he was the only one left, and yet he still stood there, feeling drained and beaten.

"Andrew?" his mother called from the doorway.

His eyes fell on the pew where Maggie had been sitting.

She had left her fan, and he picked it up and slipped it into his pocket.

The drive home was quiet and uncomfortable. He knew his mother guessed what had taken place with Maggie, but Hick was unwilling to discuss it. He didn't want to think about it, but hard as he tried he couldn't push Maggie or the image of the baby from his mind.

Later, while the women finished dinner, Adam and Hick fixed the porch step. They were in their undershirts, their foreheads glistening with tiny droplets of sweat as they removed the rotten step. It was hot for June, the screen door was open, letting in any breeze that might whisper, the windows open, wide and beseeching. Benji, Adam, and Pam's nine-year-old, came bounding up as they worked. "Is it true someone killed the baby in the slough, Uncle Hick?"

Hick paused in his hammering and glanced at the boy. "We'll have to investigate and try to figure that out."

"Daddy says they did," Benji contradicted.

Adam's slow, relaxed smile covered his face. "I said the coroner says they did. That's why we have to do the investigation."

"The kids is all afraid to fish up there now. They say the place is haunted."

"You tell the kids the place ain't haunted," Adam told his son. "That baby ain't coming back. Y'all are old enough to know better."

Benji whispered, as if afraid something spectral might hear him, "They say she's lookin' for her head."

"I'll take you fishing up there next Saturday if you like,"

Hick offered. He loved to fish and spending time with his nephews was one of his favorite pastimes. "We'll go to our secret spot and show them all how foolish they're being."

Benji stood quietly, considering. After a pause, he replied in a small voice, "I'll go if you think it'll be okay."

"You don't have to be scared of anything. I promise."

The boy seemed satisfied, and Hick watched him run to tell his brother Henry, who was standing beside the propane tank scratching a mosquito bite. It wouldn't be long until the other boys, the little one stuck in the playpen and the infant sleeping on his mother's bed, would be joining them. Three of these boys were Adam made over, stocky, wide-shouldered and easy-going with ready smiles and snapping dark eyes. Henry, the second son, could have been Hick's child. He was thin and pale, tall with long limbs and blue eyes. Their constantly growing family kept Adam and Pam preoccupied and happy.

After dinner, Hick sat alone on the porch swing. In spite of the love he felt for his nephews, there were times he needed to step outside into the quiet. He had just lit a cigarette, when the screen door swung open and his sister appeared. "I see you're smoking."

"And?"

"You only do that when something's wrong." She sat beside him on the swing. They'd always been close, despite the eight years between them. There had been another brother, but he had died before Hick was born. As they were growing up, Pam fully believed Hick belonged to her, like a puppy or kitten, and she mothered him. It was her idea for

Adam to get Hick on at the sheriff's office as deputy when he came back from the war. She pushed a blonde tendril out of her eyes and looked into his face. "Can you talk about it yet?"

This was a game they had played since childhood. When anything bothered Pam, it came right out, sometimes angrily, sometimes hysterically, but it was never a secret. With Hick, things weren't so easy. It would sometimes take him weeks to be able to talk about what was on his mind. Since the war, he couldn't talk at all.

He took a long draw from his cigarette and shook his head. "Not yet."

It was getting on toward evening when he found himself driving toward the slough. After the muggy summer day, the air nearly buzzed with electricity. Heat lightning flashed in the distance. He parked the car and walked to the edge of the water, sitting in the rustling grass and listening to the crickets. The place where the baby had been found was invisible from this vantage point, as if that little corner of the slough didn't exist. Lightning bugs rose from the ground all around him and occasionally a fish would jump, making a meal of one of the countless mosquitoes that hovered above the water. He pulled Maggie's fan out of his pocket and smelled it. Her perfume lingered, heavy and sweet, just as it used to linger on his clothes after they'd been together. A sudden warm gust of wind sprang up, bringing the distant sound of thunder.

"Howdy, Sheriff," a voice said, making him jump. He glanced up to see Iva Lee Stanton, a wispy sixteen-year-old with wide blue eyes. He remembered her from before he went to war. She was a bright, bubbly girl with braids and one front tooth. That was before she jumped out of the hayloft on a dare and knocked herself senseless. Now the kind people called her daft, but most called her an imbecile.

He rose, brushing the dirt off his pants. "Howdy, Iva Lee. What you doing out by this slough so late? Sun's about to go down. Does your daddy know where you are?"

She looked at him with those blank eyes, and it made a shiver run down his spine to think of a mind so vacant and unpredictable.

"No."

"You need to get home … it's almost dark. You could fall in the water and then what would happen to you?"

She frowned, knitting her eyebrows and jutting her lower lip out.

Hick was annoyed by the girl interrupting his thoughts. More irritably than he meant, he told her, "I don't want you out here at night, you hear? You come on, I'll take you home."

She frowned and stomped to the car.

Hick started it and turned toward the road. "You spend a lot of time up here in the last few weeks? Or seen anyone actin' funny?"

"No," she said with a sullen face. "Daddy don't like me out much."

"Well, you best listen to your daddy and keep to home."

Iva Lee turned toward the window, evidently not pleased with the suggestion.

He pulled into the driveway and saw Bill Stanton coming from the barn with a shotgun and lantern. His face clearly showed relief when his daughter got out of the car.

"Hey Bill," Hick said, shaking the man's hand.

"Where'd you find her?"

"Out by the slough. I thought I ought to bring her home. She really shouldn't be out after dark … it's easy to get lost down there."

Iva Lee stood before her father with her arms crossed, her face wearing an awful, put-upon pout. "Iva Lee, get to the house," her father said.

She stomped her foot.

Bill raised his voice saying, "You best start listening to your mother. She's in the house scared to death. Now get inside, for Christ's sake."

Iva Lee muttered the whole way to the house and Bill sighed. "God almighty, Sheriff, what am I gonna do with her? I can't lock her up. She's making her mother a nervous wreck."

"I don't know what to tell you, Bill."

"I know that," he said with a small smile. "Well, I'm obliged to you for bringing her back."

Hick climbed back into his car and pulled the fan back out, but the warm feeling of remembering happier times was gone. He tried to conjure it back on his way home, but it would not return.

5

Hands cupped around a mug, Hick sat at the kitchen table staring into his coffee, feeling the warmth gradually dissipate. Thunder rumbled outside and the spoon rattled on the saucer, but he didn't move. He was gone, lost somewhere inside himself. He couldn't say exactly where he was or what he was thinking, as his mind didn't seem capable of forming a thought. He just stared down into the same cup he'd been holding for forty-five minutes, trying to remember what it felt like to be alive.

Lying in bed the night before, he'd hoped the rain's hypnotic tapping against the tin roof would help him get some sorely needed rest. But even that familiar, relaxing sound couldn't bring sleep. As soon as he climbed into bed, his heart began the familiar racing, adrenaline shooting through his body whenever he closed his eyes, his breath coming in short gasps, his legs fidgety and restless. It had become routine, this tossing and turning for several hours, before despair would set in and he would finally just get up. He knew he had to sleep for some of the night, not sleeping at all was impossible. But it was in short spurts, and never enough.

Standing before the mirror every morning, his routine was the same. He shaved and then combed his hair. In high school, he could never grow a mustache like Errol Flynn. The girls had always loved his blue eyes and fair hair, but he wanted to be dark and swarthy like the matinee idols he saw. His father said his hair would darken as he grew older, but it never did. It remained blond and unmanageable, requiring a generous helping of Brylcreem to keep it from jutting out at odd angles. Lastly, he slipped on his uniform, starched as always, his perfect appearance belying the insecurities inside.

Rain blew in horizontal sheets as Hick made his way into the station. Unable to face Maggie, he skipped the diner. Opening the door, he stumbled inside and took his hat off, shaking water everywhere. Wash and Adam looked up.

"You find your webbed-finger criminal?" Wash asked as Hick hung his hat.

"No, but I found a place where a bunch of kids broke bottles on the street and made a mess. You reckon you got time to clean that up?" It was spoken impatiently and made Wash's eyebrows go up.

"In the rain?"

Hick sat down heavily in his chair and ran his fingers through his hair. "No, not in the rain."

Wash and Adam exchanged glances. "Where'd you eat breakfast?" Adam asked, sitting on the edge of Hick's desk.

"Didn't."

"Come on," Wash said. "I'm buying."

"I'm not hungry."

Adam and Wash each took an arm and lifted him from his chair. "Alright, alright," he said in surrender, "I'm coming."

They opened the door. Thunder rolled and the rain fell heavily, making the gravel road that served as the town's main street a sloppy, muddy mess. Quickly, they ran across the street to the diner, their feet sloshing through the puddles. The bell on the door rang and they closed it behind them, making their way to a booth. Hick glanced up and saw Maggie talking to Matt Pringle. She was smiling, her eyes sparkling and she patted his arm as she walked past him to their table. When she saw Hick, the smile faded. "Hey boys, what can I get you?"

Adam and Wash ordered, but Hick muttered, "Just coffee," handing her the menu. She barely looked at him as she added it to the stack, and then, glancing toward the door informed them, "Doc's here," and made her way to the kitchen.

The doctor walked in, dripping from the storm and, spying the men, joined them. "Morning all."

"Hey, Doc," they answered.

"Making any progress?"

"None," answered Wash. "What are we supposed to do, ask everyone in town if we can see their fingers?"

The doctor shook his head. "You're law enforcement, use your imagination for God's sake. You ain't got to make a big to-do, just start looking at the people you meet."

Hick had been staring at the darkness outside the window. "Well, it ain't a Stanton. I was up there yesterday and seen Iva Lee and her daddy. They got nice, normal-looking fingers."

"What were you up there for?" Adam asked him.

"Oh, I went back to the slough to … hell, I don't know what I thought I was doing. Anyway, Iva Lee was wandering around up there, so I took her home."

"Why would she be up at the slough?" asked Wash.

"Damned if I know."

"She see anything?" Adam asked.

Hick shook his head.

Maggie came back with four cups in one hand and a pot of coffee in the other. "Morning, Doc. I suppose you'd like some coffee?"

"That'd be nice, hon," he said, patting her hand. She took his order and he asked, "How you been feeling?"

"Better, thanks."

Hick abruptly turned from the window. "You been sick?"

"Just anemic. Doc gave me some iron pills."

"Anemic?"

"It comes from not eating right," Doc said. "Ain't nobody around here got enough money to put meat on their plate every night."

Hick looked at her questioningly and she bristled. "Everything's fine."

She retreated, scurrying toward the counter, and Hick turned back to the window. He could see her reflection as she worked, wiping off the counter and setting dishes in the tub behind her. She turned back to take the order of a farmer who had just come in from the rain. The reflection of her face in the window melted into the memory of her face from years before. Then, it was wan and haggard from the knowledge that he would soon be going to war.

"Jesus Christ, Mag! Do you have to be stubborn about everything?"

She pulled a bunch of lilacs from the bush and ran them beneath her nose. "Not everything." She said it in a false, light voice that irritated him.

In frustration, he ran his hand over his newly shorn hair. "Will you ever listen to reason? If you marry me now, you'll get fifty bucks a month. Fifty bucks!" His eyes glanced over to the Benson house. "Think how much you and your mama could do with that."

Maggie stiffened a little. "Mama and I are just fine. Bud says I can stay on at the diner as long as I need to. You don't have to pay me to wait for you, Hickory. Your people could use the money, too."

He shrugged. "Dad's working. You need it more."

She looked deeply into his eyes and caught his hands in hers as if trying to will some inner knowledge she possessed. "Hickory, your daddy might not be able to work much longer."

Hick chose to ignore the statement. "Mag, I know how much you need—"

She squeezed his hands. "What I *need* is for you to trust me. Do you think you're going to get a 'Dear John' letter?"

He laughed. "Well, maybe a 'Dear Hick' letter…."

She narrowed her eyes. "You don't think I can wait? You think my love is that small?"

He sighed, recognizing the defiant glint in her eyes. "No, Mag. I just wish every once in a while you'd let someone help you."

"You having faith in me will help me get through this more than any money ever could. What are you afraid of anyway?"

He pulled her to him. "I'm afraid of you wantin' for something and me not being here to give it to you."

Lightning popped directly outside of the window and the instantaneous thunder behind it caused Hick to jump, jerking his mind back to the present. "It's as dark as night out there," Wash commented, wiping his hand across the window to remove the moist condensation and drawing Hick's mind away from the reflection.

The farmers were at their leisure today; there would be no working in this weather. Sounds of clinking silverware and laughter erupted from different spots of the room, and Maggie quickly moved throughout, filling coffee cups and chatting with the customers.

Adam watched the crowd at the diner. Lowering his voice, he suggested, "Maybe Wash could hang around in here for a day or two. Most of the town comes to this diner at least once or twice a week." Hick's eyes met Adam's. He understood Adam worried about Wash. The deputy was growing older and Adam had been hinting he should retire, although Wash wouldn't have it. He'd worked for Sheriff Michaels for his forty-year tenure and he intended to stick around as long as he could.

Hick quickly agreed. "Just to talk to folks … or to listen.

Something out of the ordinary had to happen. You don't just up and find a baby nobody wants to claim without something happening."

"It's so strange," Adam said. "It's like it came from nowhere. Everyone who was expecting is either still expecting or they have a baby. It's like she just showed up. And I didn't find anything out by the slough when you and Doc were at the inquest," Adam went on. "Nothing unusual at least. No recent tire marks save ours. Of course that part of the slough has always been quiet unless you're aimin' to fish. I wonder if anyone heard anything. Maybe they thought it was an animal."

"I reckon after the rain stops, we could check with the people living near by," Hick ventured. "Ask them if they seen any strangers wandering around."

The wind blew a gust of rain against the window and thunder crashed loudly. The farmers glanced up uneasily. There was a momentary silence, but seeing no signs of hail, the conversations began again.

Hick put his cup back on the saucer and voiced what they were all thinking. "I have a bad feeling we're all just wasting our time on this." This was met by silence.

Maggie's laughter drew their attention. She was standing beside Matt Pringle, and he was turned on the stool facing her. He was smiling, his hand possessively on her elbow. Hick squirmed involuntarily, and at once, felt Adam's eyes upon him.

The bell on the door rang again and Fay Hill entered. All of her motions seemed designed to attract the least amount of attention. She crept across the room and spoke with Maggie, and soon had a cup of coffee. Though Fay and Maggie were the same age, Hick couldn't help but notice a difference. Maggie had changed little since high school, but Fay was faded and worn, like a comfortable work shirt. Her husband, Tobias Hill, had been Hick's best friend in high school, but the war had changed him.

Beside her, as was often the case, was her son Bobby. Maggie handed the little boy a donut and patted his head as he smiled up at her in return. "He looks more like his daddy every day," Adam commented. The boy had been born while Tobe was in Europe. There had been no more children, because these days Tobe's passions tended to lean more toward a bottle of Jim Beam.

Fay worked every day at the post office because her husband was rarely sober enough to earn a salary. She smiled at the men as she passed their table on the way out. She had been the prettiest girl in school, twice voted "Cotton Queen," and no one was surprised when she fell for Tobe, a star athlete, good looking with an easygoing, charming manner. They had been the perfect couple, graced with beauty and luck. Now, Tobe kept company with ghosts and entertained them with whiskey.

Hick watched her run across the street, her coat held over her head to keep the rain off. The door had barely closed behind her when Lem Coleman, a snub-nosed farmer with red skin and eyes that squinted permanently from hours in the sun, approached the table. He owned a large amount of property five miles from town in the farming community of Ellen Isle.

"Morning all," he said in his friendly farmer's drawl.

"Hey, Lem," Adam replied, shaking his hand.

Lem removed his hat. "Boys, I sure wish you could do somethin' about Tobe. He commenced to shooting again last night at about one in the morning. The missus is convinced he's gonna kill us all in our sleep."

"I reckon we're gonna have to finally lock him up," Wash commented.

"No," Hick said quickly. "Do you know how embarrassing that would be to Tobe … and Fay for that matter?"

"Listen, Sheriff," Lem told him, "we know what a big shot Tobe was in high school, but the truth of the matter is he ain't nothing now but the town drunk."

Hick's eyes narrowed and he opened his mouth to say something when Adam interrupted.

"Lem, we'll try to confiscate Tobe's gun. Would that satisfy you?"

Lem nodded and turned to Hick. "I ain't got nothin' against the boy. I just don't want to see anyone get hurt."

"I know, Lem," Hick answered, his anger extinguished by the reality of the dangerous game Tobe was playing.

Lem shifted his feet and asked, "Y'all got any ideas about that baby, yet?"

"We got a few leads," Adam told him.

"Well, I wish you luck," Lem told them, putting on his hat and rushing out into the rain.

After he left, Adam turned to Hick. "If Tobe don't stop firing that gun, you know we're gonna have to lock him up."

"I realize that," Hick answered with a sigh.

Soon Maggie arrived carrying three plates heaped with eggs and grits. Turning to Hick, the doctor asked, "You already eat?"

He shook his head. "I'm not really hungry. If you'll excuse me, I got some work to do."

The doctor rose and let him out and Hick walked out into the rain without looking back. As the drops smacked him in the face, waking him, his thinking cleared. He recalled the grisly image of the baby lying on the table. In his mind, he heard the wail of a newborn infant so audible that his steps halted. There was no comfort in the cry; it was the desperate cry of the powerless. He crossed the street and went to the newspaper printer.

"Wayne?" he called as he opened the door.

Wayne Murphy came from the back room wearing a leather apron covered with ink. Hick hated Wayne's open criticism of his job as sheriff, but now was not a time for pride.

"What can I do for you?" Wayne asked, wiping his blue hands on a towel.

"Can you get me the back issues of the paper for about the past month?"

"No problem." Wayne walked to a large metal filing cabinet that sat beneath two wide windows covered with Venetian blinds. He opened a drawer and started counting out the weekly editions.

"Better make that the past six weeks," Hick decided.

Wayne kept thumbing through files, got the papers, and stacked them neatly by pounding them on the top of the cabinet. He handed them to Hick.

"Why do you need these?"

Hick pulled his hat down over his eyes and turned to leave. "I need help sleeping at night," he answered bitterly and put the papers under his jacket before he ran back out into the rain.

6

The papers sat neatly on his desk, waiting for the long hours in the night when sleep wouldn't come. The storm had passed and Hick gazed out the window lost in thought. His head ached from lack of sleep and food, as well as the uncertainty of how to conduct the investigation. He watched Adam and Wash cross the street, trying to avoid puddles. They opened the door and stepped in, bringing the smells of rain and bacon with them.

Hick stood. "Adam, you ready to go out toward the slough? Start asking questions?"

"Sure," Adam said, grabbing up his hat. "Wash can hold down the fort."

"Good luck," Wash said, settling in at his desk. "Only way to figure this thing out is leg work."

Hick and Adam drove out toward the slough, the windows down, letting in the rain-chilled air. Everything felt moisture-laden, even the seats of the car felt damp. The clouds hung low and gray over the flat delta, threatening to dump a new round of precipitation at any moment.

"Let's start at the Thompsons'," Adam suggested.

The Thompson household was at the far end of the slough. Adam's son, Benji, spent a lot of time with Jack Thompson, his best friend.

"Yeah, I'd like to get that one over," Hick agreed remembering his last visit to the house. "Poor old lady."

Claire Thompson had been sitting on her porch swing the last time he stopped at the house, barely a month ago. It had been a hot day for May and the air already had that bright, summer feeling. A beautiful day to deliver such horrible news—her only son, Ross, was dead.

"What a day." Adam shook his head as if reading Hick's thoughts.

"I never thought Ross would die so young. He was always so cautious."

"And now those boys are orphans."

Claire's only child, Ross, had fallen asleep at the wheel of his truck and driven off a bridge. His wife had died four years earlier in childbirth, and now his aged mother was raising their boys alone.

Adam drove the car up the two sandy dirt lines in front of the house and parked beside the propane tank. The house stood stark and white, almost cruel in its sterile perfection. Mrs. Thompson raised no flowers or trees, saying there was no money to be made in prettying up the place. John and Claire Thompson had risen from the abject poverty of sharecropping to owning one of the largest farms in the county.

After John died, most of the land was rented out. In spite of her advanced years, Claire kept busy with a sizable garden and chickens. She didn't believe in being idle.

Claire came out to meet them, wearing a tan work dress with dainty flowers sprinkled unconvincingly on it. Those flowers did nothing to temper the severity of the austere platinum knot that bound her hair.

Moving with amazing alacrity for a woman of her age, she met them as they climbed from the car. "Morning, boys."

Both men removed their hats. "Morning, Miss Thompson," Hick said. "How have you been?"

"Well, I'm getting by. Jack and Floyd keep me on my toes, no doubt about that. Ain't been the same around here since Ross passed."

Hick noticed the water-logged pickup still standing right in the yard where the tow truck had left it. He swelled with sympathy for the woman.

"You know if there's anything we can do to help, we'd be glad to."

She squeezed his hand. "I know that, Hick. You were always such a good boy. Your daddy was so proud of you."

"Ma'am, if you don't mind, Adam and I would like to talk to you for a moment."

She seemed surprised. "By all means. Please, come in."

The two men followed Claire up the porch steps and into the house. Unlike his sister Pam's house, where there was always a baseball glove or roller skates lying on the table, everything here was perfectly neat, not one item out of place, not a speck of dust anywhere. It was hard to believe two small boys lived there. They passed by an ancient grand-father clock that stood in the foyer and went to the sitting room. Turning to Adam, Claire said, "Thank you for having Jack over last weekend. He loves being at your house."

Adam grinned. "He's a good boy. You're doing a heck of a job with them kids."

She seemed to shrink a little. "I wish I didn't have to."

Hick sat on a chair, his hat in his hands. He absentmind-edly turned it and asked, "Ma'am, if you don't mind, we'd like to ask you a few questions pertaining to the child we found in the slough."

Claire's eyebrows went up. "Oh?'

Adam leaned forward. "With you living so near, we thought you might have seen or heard something. We're having a devil of a time."

She folded her hands and placed them in her lap with her lips pursed in thought. "Really boys, I don't know how much help I can be. There's always kids up around that end of the slough. Teenagers come up in their cars."

"What about strangers?"

"Oh, I ain't seen no strangers wandering around there. I keep an eye open for that, me being alone and all."

"Has there been anything at all odd up there? Anything out of the ordinary?" Adam wondered.

She smiled a little. "The only thing out of the ordinary is there ain't been as many little boys fishing this past week. Jack says they're afraid."

Hick shook his head. "Kids get the damndest fool notions in their brains. What about these teenagers in their cars?"

"Well, they come up here for … alone time, if you know what I mean. Not just schoolboys, either. Some young men bring their ladies up here, too."

Hick pulled out his notebook. "Hate to ask you this, Miss Thompson, but could you give me any names at all? Anyone you seen around the slough the past month?"

"I don't want to seem like a nosy old biddy," Claire said a little jokingly. "But you know I do keep a watchful eye around here at night. Especially since Ross died. I ain't particularly comfortable being all alone way out here, but I hate to leave my home."

Adam reassured her saying, "No one thinks you're being nosy. Perfectly understandable, you being in the position you're in. I'd probably be keeping an eye open myself."

Unconsciously, Hick imitated Claire's posture, absolutely straight and motionless. She grew up in an age of corsets, and her posture was unbending and rigid. After a slight hesitation, she began, "I seen Buck Hearn and Lida Webber one night last week. Her daddy would tan his hide if he knew, too. I seen Sam Logan's car, Jimmy Allen was with Rachel Kellum, Matt Pringle was walking with Maggie Benson, and Dick McCarter was with Betty Harmon. I know all those kids, none of 'em would have done what you're asking about."

Hick had written down the names without showing any emotion, other than a faint blush when Maggie's name was mentioned. He wondered if he'd ever get that under control. He looked up after writing and noticed Adam looking at him keenly, but he avoided his gaze and turned his attention back to Claire.

"What about animals?" he asked her. "You got any panthers or coyotes running around you know of?"

"No panthers. Sure, there's always coyotes, but I don't see 'em down at the slough."

"Anything else? Hear anything?"

Claire shook her head. "Johnny's up there a lot. But he always has been. It's where he gets his supper."

"Johnny's just fishing, right? You didn't see him prowling around, acting odd did you?"

"Oh no." Claire began. "Well, of course he was acting odd. It's Coal Oil Johnny. But nothing unusual."

Hick read over the list again. Coal Oil Johnny was the town hermit. He lived in a shack way out in the sunken lands and came to town twice a month for coal oil. It was what he used for cooking, heat, and light. He was not likely the person they were looking for, but he might be someone with information. He jotted his name with a notation to interview him. Closing his book, he said to Adam, "You got anything else? That about does it for me."

Adam shook his head and rose. He paused on the porch telling Claire, "Let us know if you need anything, ma'am. Won't you?"

Her eyes welled a little and she patted Adam's shoulder. "I do appreciate all you've done for me and the boys. I know Ross would be grateful."

Finding no one home at the Pringle's or the Scott's, the two men drove back to town. Light was beginning to break through the thinning clouds, patches of blue amidst the gray, dissolving before the sun's brilliance. After a prolonged silence, Adam said, "I'm sorry you had to find out about Maggie that way. I was going to tell you."

"Tell me what?"

"She's been seeing Matt pretty steady now for a couple of months."

"I don't know how it could possibly matter to me."

"Dammit Hick, anyone with eyes can see you two belong together. She waited for you and wrote to you faithfully for three years while you were gone, and the best you can do for her is get back and break the engagement. You couldn't even come up with a decent reason."

"People change," Hick remarked.

"No," Adam argued. "You didn't change. Boy, if there's one thing you're bad at, it's lyin'. No one gets it … your sister, your mother. You and Maggie were meant to be together. Hell, you've been inseparable since you were born."

Hick looked out the window at the sodden fields. He closed his eyes and the image of a bloody farmhouse flitted before them, frightening in its vividness. He shuddered. "Adam, you wouldn't understand."

"Goddammit, I hate that answer! No one understands and no one ever will because you came home and shut the door. Why don't you tell someone what's wrong … work it out. You need her, Hick."

Hick pulled a cigarette from his pocket and cupped a hand over it while he lit it. "She's moved on, Adam. So have I. Why can't everyone else?"

"Because you're either a liar or a fool if you think either of you has really moved on. Don't you see how her face lights up when you walk into that diner? Don't you see how her eyes never leave you while you're there, and how they follow you to the office every morning? Please tell me you're not that dimwitted, boy!"

Hick leaned back in the seat and took another drag from the cigarette, pulling his hat down far over his eyes. "Well, now she's got Matt to comfort her, and I've got the support of my loving family. Let it go, Adam. For God's sake, please let it go."

Neither man said another word until they got back to town, the passive silence thick and heavy, a precarious levee barely holding back a deluge of disagreement.

7

The red plastic ashtray was heaped with the remains of last night's sleeplessness. Ashes spilled down the sides like sand on a windswept dune, smudges of white splattered against the dark wood of the table, and Hick absentmindedly ran his fingers over them, blurring and smearing the little dots, leaving only a vague, gray haze. He tried to recall when he had finished the pack. In the war, Lucky Strikes had been part of his C-rations and had helped to pass the many hours of tedium, had helped take his mind off the fact that his father had died and he had not been home to bury him.

His father had been one of those larger-than-life men that sons look up to in awe, but he had also been a loving man, and as the school principal, had been a fixture in every part of Hick's world. Every Lucky Strike lit and smoked down to a nubbin had helped ease the pain of knowing he would never see his father again, never feel a warm, fatherly embrace again, might not live to see any of his family ever again.

He crushed out another cigarette, coughed heavily, then picked up the ashtray and dumped its contents into the trash can. It was another soggy Arkansas morning. Water stood on the dirt roads, puddled in the ruts, glistening and brown in the morning's diffused sunlight. Already hot, it promised to be another overcast, summer day.

As he dressed for work, Hick thought of what he had read in the stack of old newspapers the night before when sleep, again, didn't come. Nothing out of the ordinary had happened. No gypsies spied, no itinerant workers coming from the hills to chop cotton, no one out of the ordinary had passed through town. Of course the last six weeks had held plenty of the death that goes hand in hand with poverty. The measles had taken two children, a young woman died in childbirth, an old man had a stroke, there had been a hunting accident, and, of course, Ross Thompson's car accident. None of this gave any hint as to where the baby had come from.

It was Tuesday, only four days since she had been found and yet, Wayne Murphy had been quick to point out in Monday's paper that no one in town was safe as long as this killer walked among them. Somehow, Wayne's words didn't seem to resonate with the inhabitants of Cherokee Crossing. The journalist wanted to organize a recall election to have Hick removed from office, but his calls for a town meeting had been met with silence. Hick had heard the words more than once—"Something should be done. We need to get who did this." But no one seemed to be resting the blame on him. In fact, no one seemed that anxious to find the killer.

Far from taking comfort in this, Hick struggled with the town's indifference. Where was the outrage? Instead of outrage, Hick got polite nods and timid questions. He would have preferred to have the whole damn town in front of the station with pitchforks demanding his resignation. But why should they care? After all, it wasn't their child. He slammed the ashtray on the metal draining board of the sink and grabbed his car keys.

Hick drove into town and parked in front of the station. Glancing at the diner, he noticed Matt Pringle's car out front. He crossed the street and stepped inside the café, the bell on the door chiming, the smell of coffee and bacon perfuming the air. Even that couldn't wake his dormant appetite.

Matt sat at the counter, chatting amicably with Maggie. For a moment, Hick's heart didn't beat. It constantly tried to betray him. He told Maggie when he returned from Europe he no longer loved her. For a year he had lied to himself, desperately trying to believe that the racing of his heart was due to stress, or nervousness, that the sweaty palms came from the Arkansas heat. "I just need sleep," he thought, trying to get his heart in line.

He approached the counter and clapped Matt on the back before sitting on the stool next to him. "Morning, Matt," he said in a genuinely friendly voice. With the help of a college deferment, Matt escaped the horror of war. He had married and lost a wife while Hick was overseas. In spite of what many viewed as preferential treatment, he was still well liked in town. Though spoiled and wealthy, he was no snob. A good man. He would make Maggie a good husband.

Matt shook Hick's hand. "Howdy, Sheriff. God awful weather we're having, ain't it?"

Hick agreed, at once made easy by Matt's disarmingly charming manner. Maggie approached and scratched the back of her ear with a pencil. "What can I get you, Hickory?" Her eyes stayed downcast, not straying from her order pad.

"Just coffee, thanks."

After she left, Hick turned his attention to Matt. He was a fine specimen of a farmer, tall and strong, with dark eyes and a quick smile. His degree in agriculture helped make his one of the most successful farms in the state. "Matt, if you don't mind, I'd like to ask you a few questions about the baby we found up at the slough."

Matt took a drink and sat the cup back on the saucer. "Anything I can do to help."

Maggie brought the coffee and Hick poured in a drop of cream watching it curl in the black liquid before it dissolved. "In the past month or so, did you hear anything out of the ordinary or see anyone prowling around the slough?"

Matt crossed his arms and glanced at himself in the mirror behind the counter. After a moment, he answered, "I ain't heard anything strange. Generally, if I sit on my porch, I'll see people wandering around 'cause my side of the slough is the one you can get at easy by car. The kids'll traipse around to fish or gig for frogs, but the men, they just come sit on the sandy bank where it's nice and even and you don't have to step through water."

Maggie filled their coffee cups and Matt asked her, "You

seen anything funny up by the slough when you've been over?"

Hick envied her for her dark complexion that didn't flush red whenever she was distressed. Still, he had known her long enough that he recognized the faint downward turn of her lips that accompanied unpleasant, uncomfortable feelings. "I don't remember seeing anyone. It's been pretty quiet up there for the past week."

Hick shook his head. "The kids are afraid."

"Afraid?" Matt cried. "Of what?"

Hick shrugged. "You know how kids are."

"Not really," Matt replied, drinking his coffee. Hick watched as Matt glanced at himself, once again, in the mirror.

He reached into his pocket to pay for his coffee, but Matt caught his arm. "This one's on me, Sheriff. I'll keep an eye open and if I see anything funny, I'll be sure to let you know."

"Thanks," Hick said, grateful to leave the diner and walk out into the thick morning air.

He returned to the station to learn that Wash had found the Scott family at home. The older man wiped his head with his handkerchief and shook his head. "Miz Scott says her boy won't take his shoes off since they found the baby. He even sleeps in them. She says it's like he can't forget how it felt to step on it. He ain't been the same since it happened."

"Poor kid," Adam responded, rising and walking to the window.

"And no one heard anything," Wash said, perplexed.

"Could the baby have been dead when it hit the water?" Adam puzzled out loud.

"I don't think so," Hick answered. "Doc says the only way she could have gotten that much dirt into her stomach and airways is if she were swallowing water."

"Then if she was alive, she was asleep," Adam said simply. "It's the only explanation."

Wash shook his head. "I still just don't get it. What kind of person kills a child?"

"Someone desperate," Adam responded. "Someone who didn't want anyone to know about that baby and couldn't think of no other way."

"But how can anyone be so desperate they'd kill a little baby?" Wash wondered.

"There could be a million reasons," Hick responded in a short, tense voice.

"Reason enough to kill?" Wash asked.

"The will to survive is a strong thing," Hick replied simply, turning to his desk.

Adam approached him. "But what possible threat could a baby pose to someone's survival?"

"Maybe she was someone that wasn't supposed to be here. Or maybe she just wouldn't stay quiet," Hick answered.

Wash leaned forward, rubbing his chin, his eyes distant and perplexed. "The fact of the matter is, someone carried this child for nine months, unbeknownst to anyone, and then they killed her."

"So we need to talk to every woman of childbearing age," Hick said with a tone of resignation.

"We should start with the most likely candidates," Adam suggested. "A married woman generally don't need to hide a pregnancy."

Hick agreed. "We can start with the girls at the high school and work our way from there."

Adam shook his head. "If we start questioning their daughters, we're gonna make a whole lot of daddies in town mad."

"No need to get anyone riled. We'll check absentee records. They might tell us something," Hick suggested.

"School's closed right now, but Gladys should be there," Adam stated and laughed. "Hell, Gladys is always there. When I was a kid I reckoned she lived somewhere in the back."

Hick smiled remembering his father's secretary. Even when he was young he believed her to be ancient. He couldn't imagine what she'd be like now. "I'll run by and get the records."

"And I'll check with the older, unmarried women," Wash volunteered. "Just talk to 'em and see what they've been up to."

"It wouldn't hurt to check with the farmers and see if they noticed anyone missing more work than usual," Hick added. "More than half this town picks and chops for Otis Shepherd and Lem Coleman. They keep records on who gets paid. Claire Thompson should have her renter's records. Those might tell us if anyone picking for them missed some work. We should talk to her again, too."

The men paused, the hard work before them seeming to

weigh heavily in the air. "I'll take the farmers," Adam said grabbing his hat.

"I'm off to the school," Hick replied.

He climbed into his car and headed toward the school-house when a man caught his attention. Coal Oil Johnny was making one of his infrequent visits into town, and Hick made a wide U-turn, pulling over to offer him a ride.

Johnny had been a fixture in Cherokee Crossing for decades, though most people had never heard him speak. He kept to himself and knew the backwoods and Cypress swamps as well as any animal. Self-reliant, he grew, hunted, or fished for everything he ate, and sold pelts to make the little cash he needed to get by.

As a boy, Hick had been frightened of him. Johnny would show up at the Blackburn house at odd hours because he was convinced Hick's father had healing qualities. Hick would hide in the kitchen and peer around the doorway listening as James Blackburn patiently chatted with Johnny, recommending he visit a doctor for his wart, boils, pneumonia or whatever ailment was bothering him at the time. Johnny, of course, would never go, believing that James Blackburn's touch would do him more good than all of the medicine Jake Prescott could prescribe. Still, Hick's father was unfailingly gracious and respectful to the old man. Generally, Johnny would stare at a person without answering if they tried to speak with him, but, because of Hick's daddy, he accepted the offered ride.

Now, Hick no longer feared Coal Oil Johnny. Instead, he regarded him as a man to be pitied; ignorant and backward.

As Johnny climbed into the car, Hick wrinkled his nose and glanced in disgust at the filthy clothes and long, snarled hair.

"Hey, Sheriff," Johnny said in a thin voice.

"How you been, Johnny?"

"Gettin' by," he replied showing his odd, toothless smile.

Glancing at the empty tin can, Hick ventured, "Goin' to get your coal oil?"

Johnny nodded, staring out the window. Hick noticed a flea jump on Johnny and the old man caught it between his forefinger and thumb, crushing it with his fingernail and flicking the carcass out the open window.

"I hear you've been up at Jenny Slough quite a bit lately. You see anything strange while you were up there?"

A change came over Johnny instantly. The color drained from his face and his hands began to shake. He turned his eyes to Hick. "Why you ask?"

"Just been some goins' on I'm looking into. Found a little baby up there in the water and we're looking to find out where she come from."

Johnny's eyes darted left and right in the squad car. He seemed almost disoriented, and his lips trembled around his toothless gums. "It was the eephus," he said in a whisper.

Hick was surprised by the fear in Johnny's voice. "What?"

"The eephus," he said a little louder. "I seen the eephus with a baby up there." His voice raised a little and he cried, "The eephus ate the baby."

"Nothing ate no baby," Hick said trying to calm Johnny.

Johnny grabbed Hick's arm so hard the squad car lurched violently to the right, almost landing them both in the ditch. "Jesus, Johnny!" Hick exclaimed. He pulled the car over. Johnny's eyes were wide, his face contorted with fear. "Tell me exactly what you saw."

Johnny rubbed his long, wrinkled hands together, the dry skin flaking onto his lap. He licked his lips and began, "I was up there long about three weeks ago looking for coons. I was walking through the cypress swamp as quiet as can be when I heard it … the eephus was singin'. I come to the edge of the trees and saw it there in the moonlight. It was in the water, washing that baby so's it could eat it. I knew right what it was and took to running as fast as I could go."

Hick ran his hand across his eyes. "Johnny, what did the eephus look like?"

"It was dark," he said in a small voice. "It had a woman's voice, but I couldn't see its body 'cause it was covered in a shawl that hung in the water. It didn't have no face that I could see."

"Was it tall? Was it short? This is important."

Johnny screwed up his wrinkled face. "The eephus ain't like us. It can be tall one minute and short the next."

"Could you see its hair? Clothes?"

"I only seen its shawl. It was black, like death, and it dripped down into the water like blood and it sang a death tome and it ate the baby."

"What was she singing?"

"An old lullaby. One I remember as a boy … ancient, like the eephus."

Inwardly, Hick groaned. He had a witness, but it was

Coal Oil Johnny. He put the car back in gear and began to drive again. "Why in the hell didn't you report this?"

"The eephus don't just eat babies," Johnny replied.

"There ain't no such thing," Hick retorted, his patience coming to an end.

"You don't live out in the woods, boy. There's things living in that swamp that you don't know about. You think all the old ways is nothin' but foolishness." He wiped his nose on his shirtsleeve and gave Hick a reproachful glance. "They didn't even call for the sin eater when your daddy died."

Hick bristled. "They didn't need to."

"Ain't no man without sin."

Hick turned to the window, his jaw clenched, overwhelmed by frustration and anger.

"Your daddy was good to me, boy, but he didn't understand the old ways neither. He didn't know what it meant to have magic blood. He could have saved your brother, but instead he called for the doctor. He never forgive hisself for that. He should have just let it alone … all that medicine and the boy died anyway. I told him, I says, Mr. Blackburn, you just got to breathe on him. But it was all for naught."

Hick felt his stomach tighten in rage. A sudden desire to strike Johnny filled him, but he stared at the speedometer, praying the old man would stop talking.

"When that boy died, I begged him to let me send for the sin eater, but he wouldn't have no part of that neither."

Hick sighed heavily. "Johnny, can you remember anything else about the baby or the woman carrying it?"

Johnny smacked his toothless gums together and wrinkled his nose. "It was a right quiet little baby. It weren't scared of the eephus at all."

The hardware store came into sight and Hick pulled over. Johnny climbed out and then bent over looking at him through the window. "I know you think I'm a crazy old man, but they's things out in the cypress swamp that I seen, things you cain't explain away. You'll see … the old ways are best." Hick watched the withered old man limp into the store, and then he unhappily headed to the school.

8

Cherokee Crossing High School was a large, formidable brick building on the outskirts of town that served not only the children of Cherokee Crossing, but all of the smaller surrounding farm communities as well. At its prime, it boasted two hundred students and several dozen teachers.

The student population decreased in the thirties. No one knew exactly when the depression arrived in Cherokee Crossing—it was a slow-spreading disease. More and more able-bodied men were at home during the day when they should have been out in the fields. People began leaving, a few at first, and then more and more, until only those who wouldn't leave remained. It seemed as if everyone in town was waiting for something, though no one could say what.

That was what Hick recalled about his childhood, that feeling of waiting. Waiting for summer or Christmas, waiting for something to change, some small spark to ignite his spirit and free him from the commonplace. He had wanted excitement back then. Now, he only wanted peace.

As a small boy, he remembered walking from the grade school down the road to the high school every afternoon to wait for his father, the sound of the acorns crunching beneath his shoes in November, the cold air biting his nose. By the time his father finished the never-ending tasks of high school principal, Hick's face would be red from the cold and his nose running.

Hick paused on the steps where he had spent so much of his childhood. He could almost feel it again, the anticipation that began when the sun started to sink. Then his father would emerge from the schoolhouse, coat unbuttoned, hat pulled down against the cold. He would greet his son with eyes full of love.

"Hickory, if you catch cold, your mother will tan me." He said the same thing each cold day. They walked home together, the older man's arm across his son's shoulders. The two had been uncommonly close and Hick told him everything. He talked about his Sunday School lesson or his math grades, complained about his sister, gushed about Maggie. His father would simply smile the patient smile that masked the physical pain of his cancer so well.

As Hick stood in the foyer of the school building, that same smile stared out at him from the framed portrait that hung in the lobby. Beneath it was a plaque that read, "Principal James Blackburn, 1923–1944." He had been there when the school opened and worked almost up until the end of his life.

Hick had not been back in the school since his return from Europe. He was struck by the silence; he couldn't ever remember being inside the building when school wasn't in session. Little had changed in the five years since he'd been gone. The walls were newly painted, but were the same shade of yellow. The white linoleum floor still gleamed in the sunlight that poured through the glass doors, the trophy cases still held the trophies won by Hick's baseball team.

His steps echoed in the hallway as he made his way to the office. He paused in front of the locker that had been Maggie's, remembering the kisses he would steal in the morning before school. There had never been another girl for him, he'd never wanted anyone else.

He made his way to the office at the opposite end of the hallway and paused with his hand above the doorknob. He could almost hear his father's voice, resigned and unhappy, holding up his last report card. "Hick, you are capable of so much more." What would he say to him today?

He opened the door and stepped through a portal in time. Gladys Kestrel had been the school secretary for decades. She hardly changed as the years ticked by, her hair grew a shade grayer, the glasses a little thicker, but her hooked nose and thin mouth were exactly as he remembered.

She looked surprised to see him. "Why, Hick Blackburn," she said, with a smile, "what brings you here?"

He removed his hat and said, "Ma'am, if you don't mind, I'd like to take a look at last year's absentee records."

Her face didn't conceal her surprise. "Okay," she said as she moved across the room to the filing cabinets.

Reaching in, she pulled out a folder, checked the contents and then handed it to him. "I don't guess it'd do me any good to ask what you were wanting these for, would it?"

"No ma'am," he answered smiling. "I won't keep 'em long, though." He glanced at the office that used to be his father's. A peculiar heaviness settled in his chest.

Back at the station, Adam sat on the edge of Hick's desk with his arms crossed as Hick recounted Coal Oil Johnny's story.

"Good God almighty," Adam exclaimed. "The eephus? Hell, I ain't heard that word in years. My old granny used to try to scare us with stories to keep us in the house after dark."

"Well, at least we have a witness," Wash offered practically.

Hick leaned back in his chair and scratched his head. "But to have one, and then have it be Coal Oil Johnny." This was met by a grunt from Wash.

"Maybe he'll remember something useful," Adam said in a voice of little hope. He rose and walked to the window with his hands in his pockets, seemingly meditating on what he had heard. He stiffened and had barely gotten the words, "Here's Fay," out of his mouth before she burst into the station.

She was breathless from running, and her face was tight with worry, her eyes frightened. "Tobe's got his gun out again," she managed between gulps for air. "He's shooting off into the woods and I'm scared he's gonna hit someone. I grabbed Bobby and took him straight to my mother's, then came here."

The three men rushed out of the station but Adam

turned back. "Hick, maybe you ought to stay here with her, help calm her down. She's a mess."

Hick glanced back. Fay was sobbing, sitting alone in the station house. She didn't know Wash or Adam very well, and he knew she'd be most comfortable with him. "Promise me you won't bring him in," he said to Adam.

Adam's usually cheerful expression was grim. "Hick, you can't let him keep doing this. Murphy's gonna have a field day with it tomorrow as it is. You don't bring him in this time and there'll be hell to pay for sure."

"I don't give a damn about Murphy!" Hick shouted. "I am sick of caring about what he, Lem, or anyone else says about the way I do my job. It is my job until I hear otherwise, and I say don't bring him in. Let him sleep it off. He'll be fine in the morning."

"He won't give us his gun," Wash warned. "We've tried before. It just means we'll be doing this all over again next week or the week after."

"Then we do it again," Hick countered. "You don't know Tobe, and you don't know what he's been through. You lock him up and it'll kill him."

A sob caught their attention and Adam turned to go. "Promise me," Hick repeated, grabbing Adam's arm.

Adam nodded and glanced toward the station. "Take care of her."

Hick watched them leave and then went back inside. Fay was seated in the chair nearest the window with a handkerchief pressed to her nose. Her eyes were red, her face tear-stained. "What will they do to him?"

Hick pulled a chair in front of her. "They'll put him to bed. This time tomorrow he'll have forgotten all about it."

"Thank you, Hick. I know this puts you in a bad spot, but I couldn't stand it if he got put away."

"Seems to me you might be better off without him," Hick couldn't help but say.

Fay shrugged her shoulders. "Maybe. I know he drinks and curses and he ain't worth much, but he's all I got. I can't tell you how many times I've thanked God that he married me before he left. If he did to me what you did to…." She faltered, realizing what she was saying. "Anyway," she continued with a false brightness in her voice, "I do thank you for helping him."

Hick walked across the room and sat down at his desk. "Fay, I'd do anything for Tobe. I don't know how long I'll be able to keep this up, though. If he hurts or kills someone, it'll be my head, too."

"I know that," she replied, staring at her hands in her lap.

There was a pause and Hick ventured, "You really think you're better off with Tobe? The way he is now?"

Fay crossed the room and looked down at Hick sitting at his desk. "I know he ain't perfect, but he's the same man I fell in love with. You can't just stop something like that."

"What good has he done you?"

She smiled a thin smile. "No good that I can think of. But, I know what he did over there. None of you boys came back as innocent as you left. Tobe killed more men in a month than live in this whole town. He hears 'em moanin' and cryin' whenever he's alone and it's quiet. He's hurtin', Hick. How could I up and leave knowin' that?"

"But Fay," Hick reasoned, "it's dangerous for you to be there."

"No," she disagreed. "Tobe would never hurt me—"

"Not on purpose," Hick interrupted.

She looked at him and repeated more firmly, "Tobe would never hurt me, and I won't leave him alone. If the whiskey helps to take the edge off what he's feeling, then so be it. But he needs me more than he needs that whiskey, and I'll be there when he remembers."

Hick ran his hands through his hair. "Fay, I got to be honest with you, I can't sit here and let this go on forever. If it keeps up, I'm bringin' him in. How could I live with myself if he hurt you or Bobby?"

"You ain't forcing me to stay there. No one is. It wouldn't be your fault."

"But I can stop it. To just sit back and do nothing...." His face suddenly contorted and his stomach tightened.

"Hick?"

"I'll go talk to him. I'll let him sleep it off tomorrow, but something's got to be done."

"Okay," she agreed.

"He's lucky to have you," Hick told her with a faint smile.

"We'll get through this; I know it. Someday, he'll forget about what he done. It don't matter what happened there ... he's home now."

Hick rose and walked her to the door. "I'll be out to see him in two days, okay?"

Nodding, she gathered her purse and handkerchief. Then, she squared her shoulders and took a deep breath. "Well, I'm off to my mother's. Bobby and me will sleep there tonight. Like always." She paused at the door with her hand on it. "Thank you, Hick."

He watched her make her way down the street toward her parent's home.

The cigarette he was smoking was mostly gone when Adam's car came into view. Relief flooded him when he saw they had not brought Tobe with them. Adam was alone, evidently already taking Wash home for the day.

"Tobe sleeping?" Hick asked.

"Yeah,"

There was a silence, then Hick asked, "He been shooting long?"

Adam's face was dark. "Long enough to have everyone at Ellen Isle in their front yards, madder than hell. Hick, this can't go on much longer. Those people are scared, and they got every right to be. A drunk with a gun ain't a good combination."

"I'll talk to him in a day or two," Hick promised.

"Murphy was up there."

Hick shrugged, collecting his hat. "I reckon I'm too tired to care right now."

Adam sat at his desk and put his feet up, ready for his night shift at the station. "You need anything before I go?" Hick asked him.

Adam shook his head. "Nothing happened last night when you were here, nothing happened the night before when Wash was here. I don't expect anything to happen tonight, either."

"That's what Wash thought the day they found the baby," Hick reminded him.

Adam leaned back in his chair, putting his hands behind his head. Smiling his slow smile, he answered, "Don't think there's much chance of a repeat."

Hick walked out of the station glad for the end of another muggy delta day. The car windows let in the breeze, cooler now that the sweltering red sun dipped below the tops of the cypress trees. It left in its wake beautiful ripples of pink and golden clouds, and produced a night that invited one to be outdoors.

Not anxious to go home to his empty, hot house, he turned down the street toward Pam and Adam's house. It was a gravel road lined with houses of various shapes and sizes. Adam's was one of the smaller ones, bought long before he ever thought of marrying. Hick saw Pam in the side yard taking diapers off the clothesline as he pulled over.

She smiled at him as he approached, clothespins sticking out of her mouth as she dropped a diaper into the clothes basket. Removing the pins, she said, "Hey, little brother. What brings you out this way?"

Hick made a sweeping motion with his arms and replied, "This weather. Just enjoyin' the night air."

She paused, pushing her hair back from her sunburned face. "It is right nice out here tonight," she agreed. "First time all day I've been able to get anything done. The kids is so cranky when it's hot. But this," she paused and breathed in the evening air, "this is lovely."

Everything was bathed in pink, a gentle warm breeze blew up, the mosquitoes buzzed happily around Hick's ears.

Children's voices rang out from behind the house. "They playin'?" Hick asked.

"They're catching lightning bugs to keep in a Mason jar."

At that moment a shrill scream reached them from the back yard. Pam's eyes grew wide and she gasped. She threw the clothespins down and ran to the back yard, with Hick right behind her.

Following the sound, they rushed up the steps onto the back porch and found Sammy, the four-year-old, on a chair with his hand caught in the wringer attachment of the washing machine. Henry and Benji had arrived and were hollering, adding to the chaos of the moment.

"Ooowww!" Sammy screamed as the wringer continued to pull on his hand.

Pam crawled behind the machine, unplugging it from the extension cord that ran out the window of the house. Hick went to the boy, carefully extricating his hand from the wringer by spinning it backward. The hand emerged skinned and bloody and the little boy howled when he saw it.

"Hush, Sammy. Let's get him inside," she said to Hick in a trembling voice.

Hick carried the sobbing boy into the house and they went directly to the sink. Pam turned the water on and Hick held the boy's hand under the spigot, rinsing the ugly wound. Sammy cried as the stinging water ran down his hand, the blood trickling to the tips of his fingers and into the sink, pooling with the water puddled there.

Hick's eyes fixated on the blood standing in the bottom of the white porcelain sink. It spun around the drain, a circling, swirling stain that made him dizzy. He suddenly felt hot, his forehead drenched in sweat, his head grew light and everything brightened, and then the darkness closed in on him. He staggered backward a little with Sammy in his arms.

"Hick!" Pam exclaimed. She took the child from him and he sat down heavily at the kitchen table, eyes clenched tight, stomach heaving with the smell of blood burning his nostrils. Sammy cried against his mother's bosom and she stood swaying back and forth trying to comfort him, all the while her eyes upon her brother's face.

He finally looked up at her, his face white, his lips pale. "Sorry, Pam. I don't know what happened."

"The sight of blood never bothered you before."

"It's not the sight," he said. "It's the smell. God, it's horrible."

Pam looked confused. "But Hick, I don't smell anything."

"You can't smell that bl—" he began then stopped. "It doesn't matter. Let's take a look at that hand."

She brought the child over to the table and set him on it, his legs dangling over the side. "Let mommy see," she said in a soothing tone.

His hand was clenched behind his back.

"Sammy, let Uncle Hick see," Hick persuaded.

The boy looked at him, tears pooled in the bottom of his eyes, his chin quivering. He held the hand out and turned it over. The skin had been stripped from the top of his fingers and hand, rubbed off by the friction between the two rollers. It was angry and red, moist with blood. Sammy's eyes grew wide when he saw it. The sobs that had started to die down became more noisy and frightened.

"Doc should see this," Hick told Pam.

She nodded. "Can you take me?"

They piled into Hick's car and he sped to town. Sammy's crying had turned into a muffled sob by the time they arrived at Jake Prescott's house. The child's face was flushed and miserable, his nose running, his eyes red. Pam and the boys climbed out of the car. "I'll get Adam," Hick called out the car window. He rushed to the station.

Adam was surprised to see him. "What are you doing here?"

"Pam's at Doc's house," Hick answered. "Sammy had an accident with the washing machine and Doc's looking it over."

Adam jumped to his feet, his usual calm demeanor gone in an instant. "Is he okay?"

"He'll be fine," Hick assured him. "He messed up his hand pretty good, though. Pam wants you to meet her at Doc's. I'll stay here tonight."

Adam was halfway out the door before he thought to turn around. "Thanks, Hick. I owe you one."

"Don't mention it," Hick replied, but Adam was long gone.

The files of absentee records sat on his desk. As he opened the first one, his mind wandered. He could hear Fay's voice, again, saying, "If he did to me what you did to—" He shook his head wondering at women's devotion. He thought of Fay, his mother's love for her children, Pam's devotion to her boys, of Maggie. Suddenly, the image of another woman loomed before him, unbidden and terrible, an intensely loving woman. He shook his head, begging her to leave, and convulsed with pain at her memory. He buried his head in his hands. There would be no paperwork—or sleep—tonight.

9

Hick's chin rested on his hand as he took a drag of his sixth cigarette of the morning. The sky was brightening, but was still washed out in the dawn's gray light. Slivers of purple and pink sliced through the clouds like luminous fingers, streams of light arcing out across the horizon.

He had been waiting for dawn when the town awakened and everything came to life. As he slipped on the extra uniform he kept at the station, he was too bleary-eyed to wonder that his clothes no longer fit, or that his blue eyes seemed to stand out from his thin, brown face.

He finished shaving just as the door opened and Adam walked in.

"How's Sammy?" Hick called from the bathroom.

"Doc dressed his hand real nice and gave him something to help him sleep. Says it'll be a long time in healin'. Might have to go into Memphis for a skin graft if it don't get better on its own."

Hick entered the room tying his tie and watched as Adam plopped a fresh newspaper on his desk. "I told you this would happen," Adam said, his face sober.

Hick sat down and looked at the front page of the paper quickly reading the article. Wayne Murphy wrote, in gleeful detail, of the fall of Cherokee Crossing's former favorite, Tobe Hill. He seemed to take delight in recounting the minute details of the day before. *If you want to break the law in Cherokee Crossing,* the article read, *be sure to buddy up to our esteemed sheriff first. It seems Tobe Hill can unlawfully discharge his weapon in town at will, whereas the majority of us would be in jail at this hour. The corruption and ineptness must stop.* Hick read the last sentence twice, feeling his heart pounding, trying to control his temper.

"Well?" Adam demanded. "Now, what are we going to do?"

"Tobe didn't break no laws," Hick responded.

Adam put his finger on the article and pounded it on the desk. "Hick, you can't protect Tobe anymore. It's in the paper. Everyone knows Tobe fired that weapon again yesterday."

Hick rose from his desk and got his hat. Pausing at the doorway, he turned to Adam and answered, "I ain't saying what Tobe's doin' is smart, and I know it ain't safe. But Tobe don't live in the city limits. It ain't unlawful to discharge a weapon on Ellen Isle."

Hick marched across the road to Wayne Murphy's office and stalked inside. Wayne was leaning over his printing press, apparently getting ready to publish a second edition, a rare thing in Cherokee Crossing.

He snorted a little when he saw Hick. "Morning, Sheriff. Looking for a paper?"

Hick went to the counter and removed his hat. "No, Wayne, I'm not."

Wayne seemed reluctant to leave his press. "I'm kind of busy right now," he told Hick. "Need to get this edition printed before interest dies down and I can't sell them. Can you come back a little later?"

Hick ran his hand across his mouth hard and tried to choke back his rage. "Wayne, I notice your story has quite a few details in it. I wasn't there, but you wrote with so much knowledge that it made me feel like I was." Hick paused and then asked in a cool voice, "How'd it happen that you were?"

Wayne looked up and narrowed his eyes. "Let's just say there are certain benefits to being across the street from the sheriff's office."

"So, are you saying you followed them out to Tobe's?"

"I ain't saying anything," Wayne replied working quickly and paying little attention to Hick. He walked to the back room to get more paper and Hick marched around the counter and followed him.

He had never been in the back room of the newspaper office. It was filthy with ink and wrinkled papers, the smell of musty books, ink, and oil filled the air. Wayne pulled some large sheets of paper off of a shelf and Hick approached him. "I hate to tell you this, but you're gonna have to print a retraction tomorrow."

"What are you talking about?"

"I'm talking about Tobe. He didn't break no law and I

want it in the paper. He don't live within city limits, so he can shoot that gun whenever he wants."

Wayne looked unconcerned. "Sure, Sheriff, I'll print a retraction, right behind the obituaries. Won't really matter. Damage is already done."

"I know that," Hick responded, running his hand through his hair. He looked down into Wayne's face and said lowly, "If I catch you at another crime scene, I'll arrest you for obstruction. Is that understood?"

Wayne backed up a little, adjusting his glasses and standing up taller. "You can't do that. It's censorship."

"You can print whatever you want, but don't get in the way of any police work. I'll see to it that my perimeters are so large, you won't even know what county we're in. Got it?"

Wayne pulled back his lips in a snarl. "You're not doing yourself any favors."

Hick's temper was flaring and when he was angry it showed itself in careful, deliberate speech. "I don't need any favors from you."

Wayne laughed. "You sure about that?"

"We don't all bow to the god of popular opinion, Wayne. You can print whatever you damn well please about me. But it'd better be the truth."

Wayne had been bending over the press, but he paused and looked at Hick curiously. "Now that's an outdated notion. What exactly do you call the truth, anyway?"

"The facts."

"Your perception of the facts. I might see things differently."

"Fact is fact," Hick argued. "There ain't no changing it."

"Don't be naïve, boy. What if a man beats his wife? Nobody thinks that's good, but what if she's cheating on him? What if she's taunted him? That doesn't change the fact that he beat her, but it might lessen his guilt, wouldn't you say?"

"I never deal in hypotheticals."

Wayne sighed. "Let me just put it to you like this, people believe what is convenient to believe … what challenges them the least. It's easier to believe a man beat his wife because she was askin' for it than it is to believe he's just a bastard."

"So which do you do, Wayne. Report facts or editorialize? Because I thought your job was to print the news."

Wayne shook his head. "My job is to sell papers, period."

Hick's eyes narrowed. "So that's how it works? You print what will sell the most papers?"

"Now you're catchin' on. Take that baby, for instance. Sold more papers that next morning than I'd ever sold before. Not that anyone gave a damn about the kid. It just gave 'em all something to talk about."

"And you made sure that it'd be next to impossible to find the killer by reporting every goddamn detail of the crime scene in your paper."

Wayne shrugged, apparently unconcerned. "I don't report news, Sheriff. I decide what is news. I—"

"I think you fabricate news," Hick interrupted.

Wayne paused and looked at him, and a slow, cynical smile played on his mouth. "Not exactly. I don't make up stories. On occasion I may embellish them, but just to make them more interesting. Let's just say I decide what these people will read about and what they'll believe. Hell, you're lookin' at the collective conscience of Cherokee Crossing."

Hick put his hat on and pulled it down over his eyes, trying to hide the anger that was smoldering there. "You forget one thing, Wayne."

Wayne appeared smug. "Really? What's that?"

"These people aren't stupid. The truth has a way of making itself known."

Wayne shrugged. "Maybe it does and maybe it doesn't. But, until I'm proved wrong about something, I'll give them what they want. Something to talk about while they're drinkin' their coffee."

Hick walked to the door and then paused. "Don't forget what I said. I may not have locked up Tobe, but I won't hesitate to receive you as a guest of my little establishment across the street. Stay out of my way."

"Are you threatening me? That's a page one headline if I ever heard one." Hick heard a condescending grunt and he slammed the door behind him.

Hick's head was aching as he returned to the station. He hung his hat and sat at the desk, feeling overwhelmed. He thought of all the women in town who they had not yet spoken with. Writing down a dozen or so names, he turned to Wash. "I need you to talk to each of these women and get an idea of what it was they were doing last autumn, and then again, late May, early June."

"Maggie?" Wash asked looking at the paper incredulously.

"All unwed women in this town between the ages of

nineteen and fifty. Maggie fits that criteria so, yes, even Maggie."

"Jesus, nothing like rubbing it in," Wash said with an unhappy expression.

Hick's eyes closed. "Just do it."

"I finished the absentee files from the high school for you," Adam said after the door closed behind Wash. "Nobody missed more than a day or two of school."

"Damn," Hick answered. "I was hoping we might get a clue."

Adam rose. "Sorry. I'll get these back to Gladys for you."

Hick was thankful for the quiet of the station. He was tired from working all night, and drained from his confrontation with Wayne Murphy. Staring at an ever-growing pile of paperwork on his desk, he was trying to force his mind to concentrate when the door of the station flew open and Maggie stormed in, slamming it behind her.

"How dare you, you son of a bitch!"

He had never heard Maggie curse. His weary eyes could barely connect the angry creature before him with the Maggie he knew.

"What are you talking about?"

"Sending Wash over to question me. He says he has to question all the unmarried women."

"Well?"

"If you have any questions for me, you come and ask. It wasn't me, okay? Do you want to know why? Because I've been bleeding for six months. There's something wrong with me, and I'll probably never have children."

Hick stared at her, a sudden overwhelming ache beginning to squeeze his heart. "Mag, I just—"

"You just what?" she snapped. "You just wanted to humiliate me even more? What are you insinuating? That I sleep around?"

"No," he answered quickly. "Of course not. But I—"

"Stop! It's enough." She shook her head, looking down and her voice quieted. "How could you even believe I'd do something like that?" Her eyes welled with tears and her chin quivered with bitterness and sorrow.

He felt numb as he looked at her, like someone completely isolated, someone standing at a window and watching the people inside, knowing he can't reach them through the glass. "I'm so sorry."

She stared at him a moment, a tear sliding down her cheek. "At least Wash only has to question the 'unmarried' women. It shouldn't take long. I'm the only girl from our class who isn't married. There aren't many of us 'old maids' around." She sighed. "I waited for you and you made a fool out of me." She shook her head, biting her lip. "I wonder what I did that made you hate me so much."

"That's not it at all."

"What happened to us, Hickory? You never mentioned me in your letters home, you stopped writing. It was as if, at some point, I ceased to exist in your eyes. I've laid awake trying to figure out what I did that was so wrong. How I turned you away."

"I couldn't stand the thought of the censors—"

"Hickory, that's a sad excuse and you know it. I didn't

need you to bare your soul … I just needed to know that you were alive and that you remembered my name."

He stared at her, unable to admit to the pile of unsent v-mail stuffed in a drawer at home. She stood there and he knew she was waiting for a reply, but he remained mute. Then she turned and was gone. He wanted to call her back. His mouth opened and he tried, but his throat was closed, choked with regret and too many words unsaid. He stared at the door and felt as if his heart had been ripped out. Slumping in his chair, he covered his eyes with his hand, and forced his pinched lungs to breathe. His throat swelled and his eyes burned, but the pain was too intense to be released through mere tears.

IO

Though it was still dark outside, Hick knew morning was coming by the cooing of the doves that lived outside his bedroom window. He lay there, his hands behind his head, his ashtray on his chest, smoking in bed … a thing he promised his mother he would never do.

His lungs still felt pinched, as if some hand were squeezing him, trying to press out his life. Why did he make Wash talk to Maggie? The tear that stood out vividly on her cheek was in his mind. He ground his cigarette out and sat up in bed, angry with himself for ever causing her to cry.

He had always hated when there was any disagreement between them. Generally, any argument resulted in them stomping home for half an hour and then bumping into each other as they raced to beg forgiveness. Through the years, their friendship ripened to a level that forgiveness never needed to be spoken. It was appealed for by a look and given with the pressing of a hand and a kiss.

He wanted to run to her now, to meet her beside the lilac

bush that sat on the property line between the houses they grew up in. He wanted to hold her and beg her to forgive him. Instead, he sat there, finishing another pack of cigarettes and loathing himself and everything he had become.

Finally, the cardinals broke into song and a slice of gray washed across the horizon. He rose and dressed in his fishing clothes. The soft flannel comforted him. It felt good to leave the tie and dress shoes behind.

I need to get away from all of this, he thought, briefly glancing at his uniform. The baby, and Tobe, and Wayne, and Mag consumed his thoughts. The baby especially gnawed away at his fortitude. He desperately wanted a morning of peace. The wall he had so carefully constructed since returning home was beginning to crumble, he could almost physically feel it giving way. He knew at any moment it could crash down on him, crushing him under its weight. It was a selfish, thick wall, but it had served its purpose. He had felt nothing when he arrived home from Europe. No pain when his father had not been there to greet him at the train station, no hurt when he told Maggie he no longer wanted to marry her. Nothing but a calm, stoic reasoning that guided him through this obligation that was his life.

He made a pot of coffee, poured a cup, and opened the screen door to walk out into the damp morning stillness. He loved this time of day, when the dew still hung heavily on the grass, filling the air with its freshness as the sun struggled to break free of the night. The subdued night sounds were familiar; the chirping of the crickets, the frogs, even the occasional moth bumping into the porch light were things he had grown accustomed to. Back inside, he put the coffee cup on the table beside the cups from yesterday and the day before. He poured the rest of the coffee into a thermos, climbed into the already loaded car, and drove across town to his sister's.

The house was dark, the only light a dim one in the kitchen at the back of the house. He knocked quietly. Pam had never been pleasant in the morning, and with a newborn and Sammy to take care of, he knew better than to wake her. The door opened and Adam appeared on the other side, his face covered with stubble, his hair rumpled and unkempt. He crossed his arms over his chest as the chilly air met his thin white t-shirt.

"God almighty, what do you find attractive about getting out at this hour of the morning?" Adam hated anything to do with the outdoors. Unlike Hick, he didn't like to hunt or fish. He was content to stay inside the warmth of his kitchen.

Hick stretched and breathed in deeply. "It's just nice to get away from everything."

Benji and Henry scampered into the room, rubbing the sleep from their eyes. "Are you ready, Uncle Hick?" Benji whispered.

They left quickly and Hick knew that before the car was out of the driveway, Adam would be back in his room snoring. He turned to look at his nephews. Benji and Henry idolized him. He had been to Europe, was a decorated veteran and now sheriff. Hick would trade any of those distinctions to simply be Uncle Hick.

"Good fishing weather?" Benji asked.

Hick nodded as they headed out in the darkness.

"Mama wants you to have this," Henry, the younger boy, handed him a tin lunch pail. Hick glanced inside and saw Pam's specialty—oatmeal and raisin cookies. "She says for you to make sure we don't eat 'em all before lunch."

Hick noticed Benji elbow his little brother in the mirror and he suppressed a smile. The two were nothing alike. Benji was like Adam, never bothered by anything.

Henry, on the other hand, had large soulful eyes and a quiet temper. Even at seven years of age, his face always seemed to wear a pensive expression, as if he were pondering all of life's complexities and trying to make sense of them.

Hick enjoyed observing the boys and all their little quirks because he had always been fascinated with children. When he and Maggie were engaged, they argued about how many they would have. Hick always said ten was a nice even number, and Maggie would reply that he would have to carry the last seven himself. A deep ache spread through his chest at the thought that Maggie might not be able to have children. She had always wanted a family as much as he had. Henry must have noticed the shadow that crossed his face.

"Are you sad today, Uncle Hick?"

He sighed. "A little. But a morning fishing with you two is just what I need to perk me up."

They parked on the grass and unloaded the cane poles in the dawn's quiet. The sky gradually brightened, the stars faded one by one, and the moon waned and fluttered to the horizon. Even the wind was eerily calm at this hour, leaving the water still and speechless.

They hiked westward toward the Scott household, the sandy bank quickly giving way to thick, marshy grasses and pussy willow. Bats swooped down to the water in search of a last meal before dawn, and Benji ran ahead chasing frogs into the slough.

"You watch for snakes," Hick cautioned him.

Henry followed behind keeping his eyes on the ground. Once, a turtle ambled by and then a screech owl cried out causing him to jump. Hick felt a hand slip into his, and he glanced down and squeezed. Henry glanced up, grateful.

They continued to walk around logs and through the high grass, their feet cold with the moisture seeping into their shoes. The mist above the water had almost evaporated by the time they reached Hick's favorite spot.

"When do you think the sun will rise?" Benji asked.

"Pretty soon," Hick replied in a whisper.

They walked around the curve of the slough, splashing through the water, and came to the western side. Here, the water was black and dirty, rushing to the shore and then bouncing back, like the pulse of a heart. They found a sandy spot and dug holes for their poles, then sat and waited.

Henry was the first to catch a fish. "What kind is it?" he asked, shuffling around excitedly as Hick took the fish off of the hook.

"It's a bluegill," Hick replied, stringing it on the line picketed to the shore. A snake's head peered out of the water and a large fish jumped. The slough was coming alive in anticipation of the sun. A breeze blew up and the sky lightened in a golden hue. "We'll have nice, clear weather today," Hick remarked.

By the time the sun was full up and seven fish were strung on the line, Hick felt himself begin to doze. He put the boys in charge of watching the bobbers and walked up the rise to sink down against a tree. Putting his hat over his eyes and closing them, he looked forward to a few minutes of naptime.

Suddenly, it was cold and snowy. December. Belgium. He ran through the snow, his feet burning with the cold, his lungs on fire from exertion. His breath came through his lips, warm and moist, and then froze instantly in the air before him, ghostly and opaque. Occasionally, he heard gunfire in the distance and the sounds of shelling. His eyes were trained on the back of his sergeant and best friend, a stern but capable soldier from the Bronx. They were the only two soldiers left—the rest had retreated or been killed—and they were being pursued.

Hick's heart pounded with the knowledge that he would very likely be dead before the end of the day. He hurt for his mother. His father had just died and he hated that she would feel that pain again. And he was sorry he would never see Maggie again, never kiss her or make love to her, but she was young and would get on with her life when the war was over.

They scampered up a small hill and there, in the distance, spied an old farmhouse. Sergeant Brody turned to him. "We need to get to that farmhouse."

"No!"

The Sergeant looked confused. "Let's move, Blackburn!" he ordered.

Hick broke out in a sweat. He was no longer cold, he was burning hot. He began screaming at the top of his lungs and the sergeant looked at him in astonishment. "What's wrong?" his voice echoed. "What's wrong … what's wrong?"

Hick's eyes flew open. Benji and Henry sat beside him, their hands on his shoulders, shaking him and asking, "What's wrong?"

He sat up quickly. These dreams were becoming more vivid, and occurring every time he closed his eyes. He was drenched with sweat and shaking. Recalling where he was, he forced himself to smile and say, "Nothing, fellas. Just a bad dream. I'm okay." He swallowed hard and tried to hide the trembling of his hands. Pushing his hat back, he blinked, trying to clear the fog from his mind. "Catch anything else?"

"Yes, Uncle Hick," Benji answered. "But Henry's line is caught in the brush."

Hick rose, and still shaky, put a hand on the tree to steady himself. "I'll get it. Come on, Henry."

They walked to the water's edge and Hick yanked on the line. It wouldn't budge. "It's probably tangled in a tree root." He sat down and began to remove his shoes.

"Wait," Henry called in a choked voice that startled Hick.

He looked at his nephew's round blue eyes. They seemed enormous in his white, peaked face. He leaned to him and touched his arm. "What's wrong, Henry?"

"Ain't that where they found the baby?"

"It's close."

"Do you think you oughta? You know … go in there?"

"Why not?"

"Because it's where she died." Henry said, in a small whisper.

"It's okay," Hick told him, patting his shoulder.

He stepped into the dirty water, and his feet sank immediately, cool sandy mud squishing between his toes and up over his feet. He took another step and the water washed up around his ankles, dampening his pant leg. He bent down and picked up the line, following it into the brush. Branches and logs drifted along the shore and thick reedy grass. He stepped painfully on a log and cursed under his breath, then yanked, once again, on the line. It still wouldn't budge so he bent down and reached under the black murky water to find what the line was tangled in.

The water was up to his knees, so dirty and impenetrable he couldn't see his hand in it. Groping through the mud, his hand stirred up silt, causing the water to appear darker and more somber. He hated the slimy feeling of the bottom of the slough. It wasn't deep, but the water was almost opaque, the smell was putrid, and the bottom was slick and lumpy. His fingers slid along the fishing line until they came to the hook, firmly embedded in the base of a log. He lifted the log and an eruption of mud and silt clouded the water as he pulled out the hook.

Standing upright, he glanced across the water toward Matt Pringle's house and noted that all of the slough's debris seemed to end up in this corner. It occurred to him that the baby, more than likely, had washed there and could have come from any place on the slough's shore. They needed to do more looking. Too much effort had been concentrated on this one little spot.

He sloshed through the water bringing the line back to the shore, and sat beside Henry who was quiet and pale. After a moment's silence the little boy said, "It ain't right to kill no little baby."

Hick shuddered and covered his eyes with his hand. "No, Henry, it ain't right. Killin' seldom is."

Henry turned to him. "Uncle Hick, have you ever killed anyone?"

"When I was at war."

Henry looked confused. "But I thought only bad people killed."

"I wish I could explain it to you, but I can't."

Henry peered into Hick's face. "Are you sad because you killed people?"

Hick's throat tightened and his nose tingled. "Yes, Henry. Every day."

Henry sighed and they both looked back out at the water. "Do you think whoever hurt that baby is sad?"

"I don't know."

Henry appeared to be thinking, and after a short pause, said, "I wish they'd have killed me instead."

"What?" Startled, Hick turned to look at his nephew.

"That baby never got to run or play or even eat ice cream. I already done all that. I wish she could have."

Hick stared at the little boy, astounded by his unselfishness. He put his arm around the child's shoulders and admitted, "It is a right shame that she never got to do those things."

"That person was bad."

"Yes," Hick answered, realizing that although they may not be a threat to the community, there was a killer in their midst. Shame crept into his mind. In reality, the child had not been a person to him. She had been a case, a mystery to be solved, even an inconvenience, but she had never in his thoughts appeared as a living, breathing being. She had been inconsequential, someone he didn't know. Henry saw it differently.

"I tell you what," he said, trying to take the boy's mind off such dark matters. "It's about lunch time. What do you say I take you and Benji to the diner for a burger? Would you like that?"

Henry eyes grew round. "Yes, sir."

The boys chattered happily in the back seat of the car, but Hick's mind was otherwise engaged. He thought about what Henry had said, and for some reason the idea that the baby would be smiling by now occurred to him.

They walked into the diner and immediately the two little boys eyed Maggie, who was waiting on a table. "Aunt Maggie!" They rushed to her and hugged her thighs.

She laughed as they almost tripped her up. "Hey fellas," she said, good-naturedly rubbing both of their heads. Glancing up, her eyes met Hick's in an unguarded moment when he couldn't stop the love shining from them. He felt exposed, unsteady.

"Been fishing?" she asked, glancing down at his wet pants

and muddy shoes.

"Yeah," he answered, corralling the boys to the nearest booth to keep from tracking mud into the diner.

"Anything biting?"

"I caught three fish, Aunt Maggie," Henry bragged.

"Good for you, Henry. You guys hungry for lunch?"

"Yes ma'am," the two boys chorused together.

"What about you, Hickory?" Her eyes met his and the appeal was there … the wanting everything to be okay again.

He smiled, relief flooding through him, and absent-mindedly squeezed her hand. Then she pulled a pad from her apron pocket, "What can I get you, and don't say 'just coffee'."

He could smell her perfume, and her smile was invigo-rating. He suddenly felt alive and hungry. "I'd like a burger with slaw and fries and some apple pie."

Her eyebrows went up. "I'd say you were famished." She took the boys' orders and headed back toward the kitchen.

"She sure is pretty," Henry said, adjusting himself in the booth so that he was on his knees, leaning across the table.

"Daddy says you're a damned fool for letting her go," Benji informed Hick.

"Does he now?" Hick asked, amused at the perfect imitation of Adam.

"Yes sir," Benji replied. "He says there's fools, and there's damned fools and then he told mama you were a damned fool."

Hick turned his face away from the serious child, trying to hide a smile. "Well, your daddy is usually right about these things." He couldn't stop himself from glancing, once more, at Maggie as she went back to the kitchen. And then his mind drifted back to the image of the slough. I need to see Adam, he thought to himself while the boys chattered away.

II

"God almighty, I hate it down here!" Adam complained, swatting a mosquito from his neck.

Hick removed his hat and wiped the sweat from his brow with his sleeve. He put the hat back on, squinted into the bright sunshine, and studied the bank of the slough. Mosquitoes hung in the air like wispy little black clouds, their buzzing loud and monotonous. The air was heavy, laden with moisture, giving one the impression of drowning on dry land.

"Dammit!" Adam swore as his boot sunk into the mud. He pulled his foot up, but the book stuck fast sending him stumbling, his dry sock plunging into the wet marshland. "What are we looking for anyway?"

Hick squatted on his haunches and gazed at the shoreline. "I don't know."

"Why in the hell do we need to traipse through this swamp?" Adam complained. With a frown, he pulled the boot out of the mud and limped over to a log, sitting down and putting it back on. A cottonmouth slithered by on top of the water and Hick watched its graceful movements, fascinated with the seemingly effortless motion and the elegant ripples it left in its wake. He wondered what it would be like to glide effortlessly on top instead of constantly feeling like he was being pulled down and sinking.

"Next time it's Wash's turn," Adam decided, tying his boot laces in a double knot. "I don't know how you can stand this."

"The heat never bothers me," Hick told him and involuntarily shivered. "Just the cold."

They walked along the bank, the tall cypress trees regarding them not as trespassers, but as merely insignificant passersby. They had stood unmolested in this bayou for hundreds of years and would be there long after Hick and Adam were gone.

They walked up a small rise in the land and came out near the home of Matt Pringle. Further away stood the Scott house and Claire Thompson's.

Adam paused and examined the flat piece of ground overlooking the slough, the place teenagers referred to as "pecking pond." Grinning, he said, "Remember the first time I caught you and Maggie up here? I almost ran you in."

Hick laughed and replied, "You knew better. I'd have told the sheriff you were the one who told me about this place."

"God, your dad used to hate me," Adam remembered, standing tall and taking his hat off to wipe his neck and head with a handkerchief.

"He didn't hate you," Hick argued. "He just thought you were a little old for Pam, that's all. If he'd have known you ever had her up here, he would have hated you and he might have killed you."

"I never did nothing to be ashamed of with her. I knew better. Besides, she wouldn't have it."

Hick didn't look at Adam. He remembered Maggie's soft, olive skin, pale in the moonlight. Adam might not have anything to be ashamed of, but Hick certainly did.

Adam was lost in his reminiscing. "The first time I brought Pam up here, she just stared me down like I was crazy. She said, 'What do you think you're doing, Adam Kinion?' I told her I wanted to look at the full moon and it was pretty rising over the slough. It really was … I wasn't putting her on. I knew then I wanted to marry her. It didn't matter to her that I was eighteen years older than she was. She knew her own mind, and I loved her for it."

"She always was a bossy old nag," Hick agreed, laughing.

"Boy, that's my wife you're talking about," Adam warned him with a grin.

Hick walked back to the slough. From there he had a perfect view of most of it except the corner where they had found the baby. It lay around a bend, shielded by thick grass and dense forest. The two men stood before the water.

"This is the most likely spot," Adam remarked. "It's close to the road and there's easy access to the water."

Hick looked around and then nodded. "Johnny says he was down by Scott's property line. He would have had a clear picture of the water if they were around here." The rise where the cars parked was about fifty yards away. He could see how someone could easily pull up there at night, sneak down to the water and drop the baby in. He felt his body shuddering and said in a shaky voice, "And they just left her in the water."

"Are you okay?" Adam asked him.

Hick was not okay. He closed his eyes as a wave of nausea washed over him. "Maybe the heat is bothering me, after all," he said feebly. The sound of an infant crying was roaring in his ears. He could hear it louder than Adam, who was talking to him.

"What's wrong?" he finally heard Adam ask.

Hick took a couple of deep breaths and the sound of the crying died away. He exhaled loudly and opened his eyes wide, recalling where he was and what he was doing. He was sweating, more from the distress of his mind than the heat. Adam was looking at him closely and he knew he must offer some explanation.

"Sometimes I remember things I saw … you know, things from the war. I can't stop 'em. I'll be okay."

Adam looked unconvinced. "How often does that happen?"

"Not very. It's just since this baby—"

"You tell anyone? Like the doc? Listen, we all know you're not sleeping."

"I'm fine," Hick said, his eyes on the mud.

"Hick, don't forget, I was in the trenches myself. Maybe you should—"

"I'm fine," Hick said again with a look that stopped any

discussion. He stood up and remarked, "We're right here at the Thompson's. Maybe we should check with her about last season's pickers."

Adam appeared to want to say something. His mouth opened, then he merely shrugged and they headed to Claire Thompson's house. They were met by Jack, who was weeding the garden.

"Hey, Jack," Adam called to the boy.

He paused in his work and hollered, "Howdy, Mr. Kinion. Right pretty day we're havin', ain't it?"

Adam paused and took off his hat. He wiped his forehead with his shirtsleeve and then smiled at the boy. "Only if you like it hot," he answered.

"Is your Granny at home?" Hick asked.

"She's around back finding us a pullet for dinner," he replied.

Hick and Adam rounded the corner of the house and spied Claire in the chicken yard. She laid a pie plate of feed on the ground and waited for the chickens to come and eat. Then swiftly she reached down and wrenched a young male by the neck and quickly snapped it. She moved so quickly the other chickens never paused in their eating. She carried the bird with its wings still flapping and exited the coop. As she fastened the gate, she spied the men. "Hello, boys," she said and nodded toward the kitchen. "Won't you come inside?"

Adam shook his head. "We've been out at the slough. We're a mess."

She glanced at their muddy shoes and asked, "Well, what can I do for you?"

Removing his hat, Hick asked, "Ma'am, we're looking for records on all the pickers that worked in the area last fall. Did any of your renters hire local people?"

Claire thought a moment and answered, "I have to be honest with you, I really don't know. Ross took care of all the records for the renters. I wasn't feeling well at the time. He was out a lot, checking on the fields."

"Did he keep any written records, in particular records of what was paid out?" Adam asked.

"Of course," Claire replied. "The renters hired the workers and paid them, but since it was our land Ross was responsible for reporting wages. He was always very good about writing things down." Her eyes welled a little and she quickly wiped them with her shoulder sleeve. "I'm sorry, boys. He was careful, careful about everything." By this time the chicken had ceased its reflexive movement.

"I'm sorry we have to bother you about this," Hick told her, a feeling of guilt rising.

"It's no bother," she told him, and indicating the dead chicken said, "I need to put this fellow down. Give me a minute."

They watched through the screen door as she put the chicken in the sink and then crossed the room toward a large roll top desk. "May I ask what you are looking for?"

"We're just keeping an eye on all the itinerants coming through," Hick answered. "Trying to find out who was working and who was not."

She found a metal box and brought it outside, handing it to Hick. "I believe all of Ross's records are in here. I haven't had the heart to look, but I know I'll have to. Picking season is only four months away."

"We'll get it back to you right away," Hick promised. As they were leaving, they paused beside Jack still working in the garden.

"Need any help there?" Hick called.

"No sir," Jack replied. "I can do it. It's just even with all the rain, the ground's so hard this year. Granny can't even dig no more. Floyd and me planted this whole garden."

Hick watched as the boy worked alone in the heat with no father beside him. "You sure?" He couldn't help but ask.

Jack wiped his forehead. "I appreciate it, but it ain't as bad as it looks." He glanced to the sky. "Besides, it looks like rain."

They left him straining and sweating in the hot sunshine.

The itching woke Hick the next morning. That and the sensation of not being able to freely move the right part of his face. He rose groggily, stumbled into the bathroom and groaned. His face and neck were streaked with poison ivy, his left arm and hand were covered with blisters and his eye was swollen shut.

"Great," he grumbled, forcing himself not to scratch.

Adam looked the same, and Wash laughed at the two men when he saw them at the station. "What the hell do you expect when you spend an afternoon in a swamp?"

Hick hung his hat, scratching the blisters on his neck.

"You'd better stop scratching," Adam warned.

Two days later found Hick in the doctor's office, the poison ivy on his neck infected from the scratching he couldn't seem to control.

Dr. Prescott shook his head. "You never could stop your scratching. I remember when you had the chickenpox. Pam never scratched when she had 'em, but you got the impetigo. Your daddy marched you in here and I had to give you a shot of penicillin."

"I was four years old," Hick protested.

The doctor examined Hick's neck. "Let me see those fingernails." Hick obediently raised his hand and the doctor told him, "Your daddy kept 'em shorter than that. You need to cut 'em back a little."

"He cut 'em with a pocket knife for Christ's sake."

The doctor stared at him blankly. "Then use a pocket-knife. You got some nasty boils on your neck, there. I'm gonna give you a prescription. Make sure you take these every day."

Hick buttoned his shirt and began the uncomfortable process of tying a tie around his festering neck

"Hick, how much weight have you lost?" the doctor asked abruptly, taking Hick by surprise.

"What?"

"Son, if you don't mind my saying, you ain't looking too good these days. Ever since we found the baby you've been irritable."

"I'm fine."

The doctor raised his eyebrows skeptically and Hick confessed. "Alright, maybe I don't sleep as much as I should."

"Do you eat?"

Hick shrugged. "When I'm hungry."

"When's the last time you ate?"

Hick wasn't as much surprised by the question as by the fact that he wasn't sure of his answer. "I ate dinner with my mama Sunday."

"Hick, it's Tuesday."

Hick brushed him aside. "I'm eating. I just don't remember 'cause my cooking is so awful."

"You ever consider taking a leave of absence? I can't help but think there's some things you need to work through."

Hick's eyes narrowed. "What are you saying?"

"Hick, I want to ask you a question. When you came home, why did you break off your engagement?"

Hick felt the anger in him rise. "It's none of your business. That ain't what I came in here to talk about."

"I'm not asking as your doctor. I'm asking as your friend."

"Oh, Jesus," Hick said covering his eyes with his hand. Dr. Prescott had always been close to the Blackburn family. He treated his father through the years for the tumors that kept creeping back onto the skin of his face.

"Listen, Hick," the doctor said with a very serious tone. "A lot of men come home from war and it's difficult. They keep to themselves; they try to pretend they're okay and they're not. You came home and abruptly broke off the engagement with Maggie. I thought you'd come back to your senses, and I think you almost did. You were eating at the diner a couple of times a day and speaking to her and I thought it was gonna come out okay. And then this baby came along and you've gone downhill ever since."

"You're seeing things that ain't there."

"Am I?"

"What do you want from me? Do you want me to pretend something's wrong when there's not?"

"No. I want you to acknowledge that something's bothering you."

Hick scratched his neck. "It ain't a big deal. Sometimes I smell gunpowder or blood. Sometimes I remember things. I can handle it."

"What about this baby has you bothered?"

Hick began to shake. "Nothing," he answered quickly.

"Nothing?"

Hick picked up his hat. "I need to get to the station, Doc." He started to leave and then turned saying, "Please, stop worrying. I'm fine. Everything's fine."

The sunshine blinded him as he exited the doctor's office. *It's fine*, he told himself.

12

That night, Hick's dreams took him inside the farm house. Sergeant Brody's square shoulders were always in view, always leading the way. They were his anchor, his compass, he would not let them out of his sight. He motioned Hick to the other side of the doorway and mouthed the words *One, two, three*. Then they kicked open the door and the two men were enveloped in blacknes.

Hick sat up, his breath came in gasps, his body shook, and his head was drenched in sweat. He ran his hand over his forehead and flattened his palm against his chest, his heart hammering against it. It was painful, his chest swelled and tightened and he grimaced and shifted in bed. "Breathe," he said out loud into the darkness, hoping his body would obey. His lips were open, sucking in air and making his mouth dry.

The moonlight streamed into the window bathing his bed in light. His eyes rested on the quilt. It was one that his mother had made for him and it seemed oddly familiar, yet out of place. He gripped it tightly, trying to remember the feelings of comfort and security that had been so much a part of his childhood. Back then, the world was as it should be. Now, it was spinning out of control.

He checked the clock. Why was it always three o'clock? Why couldn't he sleep until four or five? He rose from his bed, stumbled to the kitchen, and filled the percolator with water.

Waiting for the coffee, he opened another of the stack of newspapers. This time he had gone back further. There were five months' worth of papers scattered throughout his house and still nothing jumped out. *Sheriff Blackburn has distinguished himself, once again, by bungling the case of the two young men who are known to have broken into the post office. The Federal Grand Jury has dismissed the charges stating there was not enough evidence.*

Sighing, Hick put the paper down and poured himself a cup of coffee. Wayne Murphy was a mercenary son of a bitch who would report trash on his own mother if it would sell a paper.

The town was so small everything showed up in the newspaper, the purchase of a radio, the installation of a new party line telephone. How could something as significant as a pregnancy go unnoticed?

He dressed, putting on his fishing clothes. It would be a day away from the station, one sorely needed. The doctor told him to stay home and rest, to give the antibiotics a chance to start working. Hick was too tired to argue the point and he knew Adam would take the doctor's side anyway. The flannel shirt was soft and comfortable, a welcome change from the irritating tie that constantly rubbed his neck. It would be good to sit at the slough, alone and unthinking, and let the day slide by.

By the time he arrived, the sun had risen. Still early, the birds sang loudly and the earth was breathing, its vapor sitting close to the ground, kissing the grass and leaving behind beads of moisture. It was one of those magic mornings where the sun and moon were both clearly visible at once, the full moon not yet wanting to give up its hold on the night.

He walked around to the back end of the slough, close to where the baby was discovered. No one would find him there, he could have a day of peace. He brought the fishing pole along for good measure, but it was not his aim to catch a mess of fish to have to clean. He wanted solitude.

He'd been there several hours and was sitting against a tree smoking a cigarette when Maggie found him. She always had an uncanny ability to discover him no matter where he was, and he didn't feel any surprise at seeing her.

"Hello," she said.

There was something uncomfortable in her eyes and he felt a sense of foreboding. She sat beside him on the bank of the slough, near enough that he could smell her. He unconsciously craned himself toward her, drinking in her scent and enjoying the closeness.

"Hickory," she began, looking down at her hands, "I wanted to apologize to you. I yelled at you the other day and it was wrong of me. I know we kind of worked it out at the diner last week, but I wanted to make sure you know I don't hold it against you. I know you're just doing your job. I'm sorry."

He threw the cigarette into the slough and turned to her. "I knew you didn't mean it, Mag. It's okay. I'm a dumb ox, you know I've always been one. I'm sorry, too. I didn't mean to hurt you."

She nodded and looked out over the slough. Then, taking a deep breath, she said, "I came out here today, because I wanted you to hear this from me, and not from someone else." She paused and then said, "I'm getting married."

His eyes remained fixed on the black water of the slough. "When?"

"In a couple of months. Doc thinks he can get the bleeding to stop for a bit. Then, if I can get pregnant it might fix things."

His heart was like a brick in his chest. It didn't even seem to be beating. He turned to her and her eyes seemed to be questioning.

"Do you want my permission?"

"I don't need your permission. I just thought, out of fairness, I should be the one to let you know."

"Congratulations," he said in an odd, hollow voice.

They sat there on the bank of the slough, unspeaking, the sobering darkness of the swamp gripping them. The words that should have been spoken hung in the air, almost visible, like they could be plucked down and understood. But they knew each other ... they both knew what should be spoken and they both knew the words would remain unsaid. It was as if the dark waters of the swamp were swallowing them, dragging them down to the bottom of the mucky water only to spit them back out. They sat exhausted, though neither moved nor spoke.

Finally, Hick said, "I really hope you and Matt are happy together."

She stood and looked down at him, her eyes unable to conceal the sadness. "Thank you, Sheriff."

She hesitated, waiting—hoping—he thought. Then, she left him sitting beside the slough, the sun barely peeping above the tops of the trees.

He sat there all day. He didn't know whether there was a fish on the line because he never checked it, and he forgot and left it sitting in the water when he finally left. He didn't remember the car ride home and wasn't sure how he made it there.

Unhappily, he saw the doctor's car in the driveway. He shut the door and walked to the house in a hollow, empty daze.

"Hick?"

He blinked. "Hi, Doc," he said in a strained, tired voice.

The doctor sat on the porch swing. "I've got news," he said in a voice that sounded as tired as Hick's.

Hick sat heavily beside him on the porch swing. "What is it?"

"I was checking my files and I came across a notation from last fall. I saw a female patient in my office and gave her some salt pills. Seems she was dehydrated and her mama brought her in."

Hick was tired and the doctor's words were not registering in his mind. "I don't follow you," he mumbled.

"Dehydration can be caused from frequent vomiting. There was no explanation for the girl's dehydration at the time. She had no fever, and her mother said she didn't have diarrhea. It was odd. Now that I think on it, could be the girl had morning sickness. A lot of pregnant women get dehydrated."

Understanding crept into Hick's mind. "Well? Who was it?"

The doctor shuffled his feet nervously. He was wringing his hands, when he muttered, "It was Iva Lee Stanton."

13

"Dammit, I don't like this at all," Hick told Dr. Prescott as they rode together toward the Stanton farm.

"I don't relish it, either."

"Bill Stanton will have your head if you're wrong."

"I know that," Jake replied. "But I need to look in that barn."

"Why?"

"Iva Lee's grown up on a farm. She's seen babies born there all her life. Where else would she go if she were to have one?"

Hick said nothing in reply, but stared out the window at the rows of cotton growing in the sunshine, an uncomfortable feeling in his chest. A honeybee splattered against the windshield, leaving a yellow streak of pollen. In the distance, a tractor kicked up a cloud of dirt.

The car tires ground to a stop on the gravel driveway. Hick paused in front of the place. It was a tidy house, Bill and Rose had raised a good-sized family and Iva Lee, the youngest, was now the only child left at home. Hogs and chickens shared a large fenced yard with the remains of melons and eggshells scattered about. Several buildings were situated in the back, their darkened wood green from mold and moisture.

They climbed the porch and knocked. Rose Stanton came to the door with a smile. "Why Dr. Prescott, Sheriff Blackburn. What a surprise. Please, do come in. Can I get you some iced tea? Coffee?"

Hick removed his hat. "Ma'am, I'm sorry to bother you, but the doctor and me wanted to know if we could just take a look at your barn."

The smile faded. "What would you want to do that for?"

"Just routine. I'm in the middle of an investigation and there might be evidence there."

She appeared to be shocked and uncertain. "Why, I don't know … I guess it would be okay."

"I ain't got a warrant," Hick told her. "If you don't want us in there, you don't have to let us."

"Honestly, Sheriff," she said in surprise. "I don't know what you think you'll find, but I got no reason to keep you out."

"Thank you, ma'am. We won't be but a minute."

Hick and the doctor made their way across the dusty drive and into the barn. It was hot and dark, it smelled of hogs and mildewed hay, and wasps buzzed in the darkened corners by the rafters. The windows were dirty and smudged and let in little light, so Hick lit a lantern he found hanging on a hook. He turned to the doctor, but Jake was already gone, flashlight in hand, looking around in the back of the barn.

"Doc, you're wrong about this," Hick told him. "She's just a child, she—"

"Bring that lantern over here," the doctor said interrupting him.

Hick walked over and saw the doctor bending down and examining something. He held the lantern up, illuminating an old cow stall. It was spattered with dried, brown blood stains. There were two brown handprints on the wall, where evidently someone had used it for support in order to stand. The doctor pointed at a mass that almost looked like cow dung, dark and dried. "That is a human placenta," he told Hick.

"Are you sure?"

"Yes, it's definitely human. Dammit," he said wiping his neck with a handkerchief. "I was right and I wish to God I wasn't."

At that moment, Bill Stanton entered the barn. "Sheriff? Doc? Is there something I can help you with? My wife told me you were out here."

Hick pinched the bridge of his nose, his head bent so low his chin almost touched his chest. He took a deep breath. "Bill, we're gonna need to ask you a few questions."

Bill's face was puzzled. "Sure, Sheriff. What can I do for you?"

"Why don't you sit down," Hick said, indicating a hay bale.

The blood drained from Bill Stanton's face. "What's wrong?"

"Bill, we believe Iva Lee had a baby in this barn a couple of months ago. Do you know anything about that?" Dr. Prescott asked.

Bill's face paled, then grew red with anger. "What the hell are you saying? Iva Lee's just a baby. You goddamned son of a bitch!" He rose angrily and Hick put his hand on Bill's shoulder and pushed him back onto the hay bale.

"Stop it, Bill, and listen," Hick ordered.

Bill breathed heavily, his face purple with rage, his eyes snapping with fury. "You'd better not come around here accusing my baby of something without proof. If she had one, where is it now? How could she have a baby and me and the wife not know it? Where's she keeping it? Tell me!"

Hick and the doctor led Bill to the stall. His eyes grew round when he saw the blood and afterbirth. "I ... I don't clean back here anymore. We ain't got cows, so I ain't been back—" He was visibly shaken. "It's not possible...."

"Bill, we need to talk to Iva Lee."

Bill's bewildered eyes met Hick's. "Yes," he said as if he were in a daze. "I'll get her."

Moments later Bill, Rose and Iva Lee came to the barn. Bill and his wife sat on a bale of hay and Hick gently took Iva Lee by the hand and led her to another hay bale. "Iva Lee, do you remember when I saw you at the slough a few days ago? Were you looking for someone ... or something?"

Iva Lee's face tightened. Her eyes narrowed and her lips were pursed. "I was looking for my baby."

"Can you tell me where the baby came from?"

"She was mine."

"Did you buy her at the store?"

"No, Sheriff, not that kind of baby. It was a real baby. I made her myself … here." She pointed to her stomach and Mrs. Stanton gasped and bit her lower lip, tears forming in her eyes.

Hick's hands shook. He rubbed his face with them. "Iva Lee, did you make that baby all by yourself?"

She smiled. "No. He helped me."

"Who?"

She blushed. "My boyfriend."

"You have a boyfriend?"

The smile faded and the pout returned. "I did have a boyfriend. He don't come around no more."

"What was his name?"

Iva Lee put her finger in her mouth. "I dunno."

"You don't know his name?"

"No."

"What does he look like?"

"He is tall and handsome. I love him."

Bill Stanton rose from the hay bale. "I'll kill the bastard!"

Iva Lee's eyes widened as she looked at her father. "But I love him, Daddy."

"Love him. When I find him—" His wife touched his arm gently and he sank back down.

"Iva Lee, when did you first see your boyfriend?"

Her eyes grew blank, a particularly disagreeable sight and she seemed to be trying to pull the shreds of her mind together. She sucked on her finger and finally, a light seemed to come on. "The first time I seen my sweetheart, I was walking by the train tracks."

"She's always sneaking off, Sheriff," Mrs. Stanton apologized. "I don't know what to do."

Hick nodded to her and turned his attention back to Iva Lee. She told him, "It was nighttime and it was hot. I had just took a swim and was walking home. He was driving and asked me if I was supposed to be out all alone at night. I told him I was swimming and he brought me almost all the way home."

Hick shuddered. "And did he, did he touch you … on your body?"

"No, Sheriff. He just give me a ride."

"But you saw him again."

"I seen him a lot after that. He was always bringing me candy and such. We'd just talk or laugh. We'd go for rides in his car. He was right nice."

Hick wrote, the words barely legible from the shaking of his hands. His stomach flopped, listening to Iva Lee talk about this man. He had to know what she was … he had to know her brain wasn't right.

She picked at a thread that hung from the loose work dress she was wearing. It came off and she wrapped it around the tip of her finger tightly, making it turn red and then purple. Then, she chewed on the swollen end. "Do you know what happened to him, Sheriff?"

"No, Iva Lee," Hick answered unable to keep his voice from shaking. "I'm sorry, but I don't know."

She frowned. "I miss him. I could talk to him real easy. He laughed at me 'cause he said I didn't have a care in the world. It's nice … I never worry about anything." She bit one of her fingernails and spit it across the barn.

"And when did you—" Hick closed his eyes and took a deep breath. "When did you and him make your baby."

"I don't know. We did that—" she smiled a small smile "—you know, a lot of times. Not at first and he didn't want to. But, Sheriff, I am a woman. I know my brain ain't right, I know everyone treats me like a child, but he treated me like a woman. He didn't want to, but I—" Her eyes turned downward. "I made him."

"Made him," her father repeated angrily beginning to rise again.

Hick glanced at him and then back to Iva Lee. "Did he take the baby?"

Tears welled in her eyes. "No, Sheriff. He didn't take her." In frustration, she put her hair in her mouth and Hick watched in horror as she ripped a large chunk of it off. She spit it out and her eyes narrowed and an expression of dark anger, much like her father's, crossed her face. "She took the baby."

"Who?"

"A lousy woman."

"A woman came and took your baby?"

The tears in Iva Lee's eyes began spilling down her cheeks. "She said she'd bring her back, but she never did." Iva Lee's hands were clenched in fists.

"You're sure you didn't take the baby somewhere and

leave it … on accident? Maybe you were going to show it to someone?"

Iva Lee's lower lip stuck out. "No, I didn't take the baby no place. She did."

"But Iva Lee, you were at the slough. Maybe you took her there and forgot her."

Iva Lee's eyes were distant, as if trying to remember. "I don't recollect leavin' her at the slough, Sheriff. Wouldn't I recollect that?"

Hick hesitated, not wanting to put any more notions into the girl's head. "I don't know, Iva Lee. Do you know why you thought your baby would be there?"

Iva Lee's finger went back into her mouth and she shook her head. Her face grew agitated.

"When's the last time you saw your boyfriend?" Hick asked, changing the subject.

"Right before I got the baby. He said he was gonna take me away and marry me. But he didn't come back, just that bad lady."

Hick drug his hand across his mouth. "Are you sure there was a lady, Iva Lee? Are you positive some stranger took your baby?"

"Yes … no," she said hitting her head with her fists.

Rose moved to her. "Stop that, Iva Lee."

Iva Lee clenched her eyes tightly, and stuck her lip out. She stopped hitting herself, but she wouldn't look at her mother.

Hick saw the girl retreat back into her mind, her head dropped and she began to hum. With that, he closed his pad and stood. Rose took Iva Lee inside and Bill followed Hick and the doctor to the car. He was shaking and visibly upset. "How could this happen? How could we have not noticed?"

"She's small, Bill. The baby was tiny. The way she wears her clothes … it's not as uncommon as you think," the doctor said, trying to soothe him.

Bill looked at Hick with the most desperate, saddened eyes Hick had ever seen. "It was the baby in the slough?"

Hick nodded.

Bill's eyes teared. "It was my granddaughter dumped in there?"

"Yes."

Bill glanced at the house. "You think Iva Lee…."

Hick shook his head. "Bill, I don't know. If you just look at motive and opportunity … a strange woman showing up for no reason simply makes no sense. I'll talk to her again, but I'll wait a few days."

"Who else could it be?" Bill asked his voice cracking. "I remember Iva Lee before … before the accident. I could have had some of that back. Why would she throw her own baby in the slough? You think he. . . ?"

"I don't know, Bill. I promise I'll try to find out."

Bill's face was stricken. "I want you to find that son of a bitch, you hear? I want you to find the coward that slept with my baby. If you don't, by God, I will."

Hick rested his hand on the door handle of his car. He sighed heavily. "I'll try, Bill. I promise."

The next day Hick learned that Bill Stanton had been to

the undertakers. He had ordered a small stone for the grave that contained the remains of the baby. It read Birdie Lee Stanton, born and died 1948.

14

Hick paused beside his car and took the last drag of his cigarette. The flame was near enough to the tips of his fingers that it burned, not painfully, but enough to get his attention and force him to toss the butt onto the ground and smash it with his foot.

He drove to his mother's, pausing in front of the house. The memories of this place were heavy and moist, hovering around him in the smells of grass and lilacs, in the remembrance of the taste of little drops of honeysuckle on his tongue, in the hot sun that burned his skin brown and bleached his hair white. He remembered when these things had made him feel virile, full of energy and vigor. Full of life.

He climbed from the car, intent on completing some yard work, and was greeted by the sight of his mother wearing her pink duster. Hick never remembered her walking around in a housecoat while his father was living, but it had become a habit since his death.

She opened the door and kissed his cheek. "I made you breakfast, Andrew. Are you hungry?"

The gentleness of the question made him nod, although, in reality, he had not been hungry for months.

She stood beside the table as he ate, rushing to bring him salt, cream for his coffee or milk. "Why don't you sit down, Ma?" he asked her on several occasions.

"I'll eat later," she replied each time.

He refused the second portions she was trying to force on him, the food he had already eaten seemed to be stuck somewhere at the back of his throat. Wiping his mouth, he watched a fly crawl across the handle of his fork. It flew away unharmed, and Hick also rose to leave.

He felt a small hand on his arm and his mother said, "Sit for a minute. Let's just visit."

Hick's mother was the great buffer of his life. If she was ever sick, he didn't know it. He had not even realized his father was sick until the doctor mentioned something in front of him. His mother always said the tumors on his face were "sun spots" or "age spots," nothing for Hick to worry about. So he didn't.

In fact, there had been very little to trouble Hick as he grew up. His mother nurtured him, his sister babied him, his father comforted him … it was as if his family had conspired to shelter him, keep him from pain.

As he looked into her open, loving face, a feeling akin to resentment stirred deep in his soul. They had not prepared him for life. How could they expect him to be a man when they had gone so far out of their way to keep him from learning what that meant?

He understood now, the heartache in her eyes when he left home to go to war. She knew what he could not—that death and pain were part of every man's existence and that hatred lurked in even the gentlest of souls, ready to burst forth in ruthlessness and cowardice.

She searched his face, and he knew she was looking for him, for the boy who left home all those years ago and did not return. She patted his hand. "I'm glad the weather doesn't seem as hot today."

"Yes ma'am."

They sat in a thick silence.

"What do you think of your little friend Maggie getting married?" she asked, trying to sound offhand.

He looked into her face. Her eyes betrayed the disinterest in her voice. They were filled with a questioning misery. "Ma, I want Mag to be happy. It's all I've ever wanted."

Elsie rose and took Hick's dishes. She set them in the sink and paused there, looking out the window. Then, turning, she said, "I'm sure everything will work out the way it should."

He nodded and rose. "I best get started before the sun gets too hot." She crossed the room and stood on her tiptoes, kissing his cheek. It was a long, lingering kiss, full of sadness and aching.

The yard at the Blackburn house was not large. It was a town lot, about a quarter of an acre, big enough for a garden, a clothesline, a propane tank, an outhouse, and since his father had installed indoor plumbing, a septic tank.

The shed that held the lawn mower was at the back of their lot, butting up against the back of the neighbor's shed with a small alleyway in between where no grass would grow. Hick would hide things there as a boy. As he grew older and Maggie became more to him than his best friend, he would bring her there and kiss her. The feeling of holding her close made him tingle all over and he never forgot the amazement he felt when he realized that kissing her was much better than playing tag.

He jerked the door open. The inside was black and hot, the lawn mower sat toward the front. In the back were countless little tools and gadgets of his father's. Old, broken hacksaws hung on the wall, license plates, fishing poles, and broken chairs. There were little projects half-begun … things James Blackburn was going to get around to and never did.

The dirt dobbers buzzed in the darkness, disinterested in Hick. He reached in and pulled the mower out. He never minded cutting the grass. He liked the whirring sound the blade made as it spun and how the grass smelled as it fell behind him, flat and neat.

A breeze blew up and he paused, enjoying its rushing coolness. The yard had changed since his father's death. Trees were growing up in the fencerow, and honeysuckle had all but consumed the small peach tree in the back of the yard. Brush and weeds grew in the corners and patches of nut grass stood out thick and high. He could barely muster enough energy to cut the grass at two houses. The weeds would eventually consume this place.

The lilac bush still grew, but it was late now, the flowers

all but gone. As he looked at the faded blooms lying on the ground, he felt hollowed out, inextricably sad.

"Look me in the eye and tell me you don't love me anymore," Maggie's voice came back to him from a time when the lilacs were bountiful, their blooms covering the bush, their smell almost sickening in its intensity. He could still feel her fingertips pressing into his jaw, trying to force him to look into her face.

"I've seen some of the world now," he mumbled, looking away, unable to meet her searching eyes. "I know there's more. I don't want to be held back."

"Hickory, when have I ever held you back from anything?" Her voice was strained and hoarse.

Anger filled him. Why couldn't she just leave him alone? She made him want to forget the ugliness of war and he shouldn't forget ... he didn't *deserve* to forget. He looked square into her face and forced the words between his lips. "I don't love you anymore, okay? Is that what you want to hear?"

She stepped back, a small cry escaping her, and her eyes welled with tears. Then, quietly, she turned away from him. He swallowed hard at the memory, and then he turned his back on the lilacs and pushed the mower forward.

The morning dragged on and he had just finished trimming the bushes around the front porch when a car drove up and he turned, surprised to see Adam.

"Hick, I hate to bother you on your day off, but Miss Stanton come by and said we need to get out to her place quick. Says Wayne Murphy's been bothering Iva Lee and that Bill's about to shoot him."

Hick dropped the hedge shears and climbed into the car beside Adam. They sped out to the Stanton farm.

The first thing Hick saw as they pulled up was Murphy's car parked near the barn, away from the house and not exactly visible from it. Then, he spied Bill Stanton, shotgun in hand, beneath a tree and quickly figured out where he'd find Wayne Murphy.

Adam parked the car and the two men got out.

"Hey, Bill," Adam said, striding toward him.

"Howdy, Adam, Sheriff. Found this critter creeping around my house and he ain't got no call to be here." He pointed up the tree with his shotgun and Hick was amused to see Wayne Murphy perched on a lower branch, looking shaken.

"Murphy, get down here," Adam ordered.

"Tell him to put up the shotgun first," Murphy said.

Adam turned a questioning eye to Bill Stanton who replied, "Ain't gonna put it up 'cause I might need it."

"See?" Murphy said. "See how he's threatening me?"

"Shut up and get down!" Hick told him.

Murphy hesitated, looked at the three men at the base of the tree and then, finally, he gingerly climbed to the ground.

"Now, what's going on here?" Hick questioned.

"I'll tell you what's goin' on," Bill Stanton replied. "I found this son of a bitch lurking around my barn like some goddamned hound dog, looking for my baby. That's what's goin' on."

Hick turned to Murphy. "Well?"

Murphy looked embarrassed. "Alright, I was looking for

Iva Lee. I wanted to interview her for the paper … try to get an idea of who her baby's daddy was."

Bill Stanton seemed to grow before Hick's eyes. "How the hell do I know you ain't the daddy? Why wouldn't you come to her mother or me first?" His grasp tightened around the shotgun. "By God, Murphy, I'll see you in hell if I get wind you're the one."

Murphy's eyes widened with fright. "Good God, Bill! Surely you don't believe I'd do something like that." He turned to the lawmen for support. "Tell him."

Hick merely shrugged. "I don't know what to make of you, Murphy. I know you ain't honest, you told me so yourself. I don't reckon you can appeal to me for a character reference."

Murphy looked disgusted. "I can't believe you think I'd sleep with … that."

Stanton was on him like lightning. The next thing anyone knew, he had Murphy shoved against the tree with his fist poised in midair.

"Stop, Bill," Adam told him.

Bill's face was purple. The veins around his temples were engorged and pulsed with rage. He turned to Hick and Adam and then back to Murphy, and reluctantly, he let the newspaperman go. Murphy's hands went up to his collar and he checked himself for injury. "How dare you lay a hand on me."

Bill Stanton looked at him, his rage clearly visible in his eyes. "That's my baby you're talking about."

Murphy straightened his shirt. "I didn't sleep with her, okay? I just want to talk to her."

"No," Hick told him. "She won't be talking to you today or any other day. She's a child and you ain't got no right to be out here. You come around here again, you'll be breaking the law. If Bill or Rose decide their girl needs to talk to you, they can bring her to your office."

Murphy looked angry. "I don't see how you can possibly tell me who I can and who I can't talk to."

Bill Stanton moved forward. "Well, if he can't, I can. She's my daughter, and by God, if I see you up here again, I'll blow your brains out. You got that, Murphy?"

Wayne Murphy backed away a little. Leaning toward Hick, he said, "You're hearin' this, right?"

Hick made no reply. He just stared at him with a blank, stoic face.

Wayne looked from one face to the other and his eyes widened in frustration. "My, God, I can't believe this! This is news, gentlemen. The people want to know what's happened … they've got a right to know."

"We don't even know the facts yet, Wayne. Until we do, no one has a right to know anything," Hick informed him.

"I could find out," Murphy offered. "Give me five minutes with her … I know how to question people, how to interview them. It's my job. Let me talk to her."

"Murphy, I'm going to give you five minutes to get in your car and be gone, and if you're not, you'll be spending a little time in the Cherokee Crossing jailhouse," Hick told him with an edge of impatience to his voice.

"What?" Wayne cried. "You're not even going to let me talk to her?"

Hick glanced at his watch and made no reply.

Wayne's eyes narrowed with anger. "You'll be sorry for this, Sheriff. I can make your life a living hell."

Hick looked into Wayne's face. "What makes you think it ain't a living hell already? You've got three and a half minutes. You best get."

Wayne made one last appealing look and then in frustration, cried out, "You'll all be sorry. I promise you that."

He stomped to his car and climbed inside. His tires spun on the gravel as he sped back toward town.

"Stupid bastard," Hick muttered.

Bill Stanton turned to Hick. "I swear I'll kill him, Sheriff. I find him up here again, he's a dead man."

"Don't you worry," Hick told him. "If there's one thing I know about Wayne Murphy, it's that he's a coward. He won't be back. Not as long as you've got that gun."

Adam shook his head and turned to Bill. "Try keeping an eye on Iva Lee. We don't want Murphy talking to her. He'll put ideas into her head, and we'll have a hard time deciphering what really happened to her."

Bill Stanton nodded. "Okay, boys. We'll keep her close. Thanks for coming out."

"That Murphy is a pack of trouble," Adam remarked as he drove Hick back to his mother's.

"He's gonna learn someday that you can't play around with people. They're more than just fodder for his rag."

When they got back to Elsie Blackburn's, Pam and the boys were there for a visit. Adam went back to work, but Pam persuaded Hick to stay for dinner. "I cooked it just for you," she told him. "It's fried chicken. Your favorite."

Hick had forgotten he'd ever had a favorite. He ate, feeling Pam's eyes on him with every bite. Everything tasted the same to him, some indescribable flavor that reminded him of dirt and cotton. After he ate, Hick went outside to smoke, knowing his mother couldn't stand the smell of it. He sat on the porch swing and Pam followed him.

"Pretty good detective work in finding the little baby's mother," she said.

He leaned back and blew cigarette smoke into the air watching it evaporate. "That was mostly, Doc. Besides, we're only halfway done."

"But, if you ask me, it's the important half. Now at least, the baby has a name. Now she's a person, not something thrown out like old tires."

He said nothing and she continued talking, more quietly, "I'm sorry about Maggie. I know you wish things could have been different, no matter what you say."

"Maybe. But things are what they are and there's no changing 'em."

"Hick, can you talk about it yet?" Pam asked in a sad, hopeful voice.

He ground the cigarette out. "Pam, remember when we were kids and Dale Roberts was selling that pony? I asked Dad if I could have it and he told me he knew I would love it, but I wasn't able to take care of it. That's how I feel about Maggie. I just don't think I could take care of her. I don't think I could give her what she needs, what she deserves."

"You never felt that way about yourself before. You've

always been able to do what you set out to do. What happened?"

He rose from the swing and walked to the edge of the porch. Down the street and across the highway was a field, rows of soybeans stretched as far as his eyes could see, ending at a tree line far off in the distance. As a boy he ran in that field. He would run until he got to the trees and rest before running back. There was no reason for doing it, just the desire to conquer. Run flat out in the open, nothing holding him back. He no longer had that desire. He turned to his sister with a weary face. "I don't know what happened, Pam." He turned to watch the sun, red and quivering, sink below the horizon.

He woke long before the sun returned the next morning, filled with dread at the thought of the day's interview. He drove back to the Stanton farm and found himself in the living room speaking with Iva Lee.

"I'd like to help you find your boyfriend, but I need to know more about him."

Iva Lee sat across the living room in a rocking chair and stared, her little finger in her mouth, her eyes dull and sleepy. "Like what?"

"Do you know how old he was?" Hick asked her, unable to shake that uncomfortable feeling he got when she was around. He was only at ease when he could predict how someone might act, and Iva Lee was wholly unpredictable.

"I don't know."

"Was he young, like about your age?"

Iva Lee shook her head, her braid swishing across her shoulders. "No, he was older than me. He could drive."

"What color was his car? What did it look like?"

Iva Lee began to play with her hair. "I don't know what color it was. It was always dark. It only had a front seat."

"Okay, good. Now tell me about your boyfriend. Was he as old as me?"

She nodded.

"Was he as old as your pa?"

"I dunno."

"Was his hair dark or light?"

"I think it was dark. Everything was dark."

"But he wasn't anyone you used to remember from school, right?"

She shook her head. "No. He ain't no one I ever saw at my school."

"Did he ever tell you anything about himself? About who his folks were or where he might live?"

"He said the only time he smiled is when I was around."

"Did he smile a lot?"

"He did at first. Then he got sad because we done that thing, and he said he was weak and weren't worth nothing. He said he 'defiled' me." She frowned. "What does that mean, Sheriff?"

"It means he knew he shouldn't be with you. You don't never let another man touch you the way this one did. You hear?"

Iva Lee's eyes grew round. "Is it against the law?"

"It is where you're concerned. I'll lock you up."

"Yes, Sheriff," she mumbled looking at the ground.

The conversation made Hick uneasy, so changing the subject, he asked, "What do you know about the woman?"

Iva Lee's dark anger shone out of her eyes. They narrowed and she said, "She was a bad person. She took my baby."

"Have you ever seen her before?"

"No."

"Was she tall, like your boyfriend?"

"Not really."

"Could she have been your boyfriend … dressed like a woman?"

Iva Lee began to laugh. "Why would he want to dress like a woman?"

"Maybe he was playing a game," Hick offered. "Could it have been him?"

Iva Lee thought it over and answered. "No. My boyfriend was real tall and she wasn't. Her voice was different."

"Maybe he was bent over, trying to fool you or surprise you?"

Iva Lee shook her head. "It weren't him. I might be stupid, but I'm sure I can tell a man from a woman." She looked pouty, like she might be ready to throw a tantrum.

"Alright, I believe you. And you can't think of anyone else who might have wanted the baby? Did he have a wife or another girlfriend?"

Iva Lee's face grew crimson. "Sheriff, he is my boyfriend! He ain't got no wife or girlfriend. He would have told me. Besides, iffen he did why would he want to take up with me?"

Hick raised his hand to calm her. "Okay, Iva Lee. I'm just trying to understand why a woman you've never seen would come and take your baby."

"I know why," Iva Lee said, with certainty. "It was because she was so beautiful."

"How long did you have the baby before she came?"

"Not very long. I had just cut the little string thing like Pa does when the pigs is borned."

"Had you seen anyone here before? In the daylight hours watching you?"

"Not that I noticed."

"Was she as old as your Ma?"

"I dunno how old she was."

"Was she about as old as your boyfriend?"

Iva Lee blankly stared at the wall as if trying to remember. Finally, she offered, "Her hands were all bulby like an old person's."

"Bulby?"

"You know around here," Iva Lee said indicating her knuckles.

"And what did she say to you?"

Iva Lee's eyes grew dull again. "She told me she was gonna buy my baby some pretty clothes, so I let her take her. She seemed right nice."

"And you're sure you didn't dream this?" Hick asked her.

Iva Lee appeared confused. "I weren't asleep."

"Are you sure there was a woman, Iva Lee. This is important. Are you sure you didn't take the baby to the slough to wash her off and drop her or forget her?"

"No, Sheriff. I didn't take her to the slough."

"Then why were you looking for her there?" Hick persisted.

"Because I want her back."

Iva Lee stared into his eyes. The expression was dull and flat, like the button eyes on a doll. Hick's indignation and pity swelled within him. She was like the Rachel of the Bible, weeping for her children. But Rachel's children weren't destroyed by her own hand.

Hick sighed. "Iva Lee, do you remember exactly what day that was? When you had your baby?"

"No. It was a long time ago."

"How is it you never told your mama and daddy about it?"

Iva Lee began to suck her finger again. "They never asked."

"But your boyfriend … he knew, didn't he?"

"I told him, but just 'cause he called me 'fatso' one night. I never got fat, Sheriff, honest. I don't know why he called me that, but he was laughing and I don't think he meant nothing by it."

"What did he say?"

"He told me I was getting rounder and I was getting to be a real fatso. That made me mad and I told him I wouldn't be a fatso if it weren't for him."

"Did he know what you meant by that?"

Iva Lee twisted her hair. "Yeah."

"How do you know?"

"'Cause then he asked me how long I had thought that, and I said a good long time."

Even the man who had gotten her pregnant hadn't really noticed, Hick thought to himself in amazement. She remained so small; it just never drew any attention. "When you told him you were gonna have a baby, was he happy?"

"No."

"Was he angry?"

"Oh no." Her lip went out in the pout that seemed customary for her. Her whole face was scrunched. "He said he was gonna marry me and make it right."

"And what happened?"

"He never came back."

"When you first saw your boyfriend, it was last summer, right?"

Iva Lee nodded.

"So, he was your boyfriend for more than a year, right?"

"I dunno. It was a good, long time."

Hick rose, anxious to be done with the interview but trying to think if there was anything left unasked. "If he comes around again, or if you remember anything, will you have your daddy drive you to town?"

He looked down at her sitting in the rocking chair, fingers in her mouth, eyes glazed, and felt disgusted that any man could sleep with such a child.

She turned her eyes up to him and said, "I'll tell him."

"It was definitely someone from town," Wash said, as Hick relayed the conversation he had with Iva Lee to Wash and Adam.

"Had to be," Adam agreed. "Or someone very nearby. An itinerant or traveling salesman would not have been around that long." He paused and then added, "I wonder if Johnny could identify Iva Lee as his "eephus" if he saw her."

"I'm not convinced Iva Lee is the 'eephus,'" Hick said.

"She had to be," countered Adam.

"Besides, no one but Iva Lee and the father knew of the baby," Wash added. "Iva Lee Stanton is the only person who could have put that baby in the slough. You finding her at the scene all but corroborates it. Whether she realizes what she did is another question."

"The way I see it," Adam agreed, "our job is to find the man who slept with her. The question of how the baby got in the slough seems to be answered. The real question is who fathered the child?"

Hick hesitated. "I reckon we need to start checking on every man who ever had any contact with Iva Lee Stanton." He paused and added, "Start with Murphy."

15

Hick lay on top of the sweat soaked sheets and tried to sleep. June's heat had been building in the house all day and there weren't windows enough to let it out once night's coolness cloaked the land. His t-shirt and underwear stuck to him, and he lay perfectly still wishing for the smallest of breezes to pass over him.

He felt a storm brewing; the sweat stood on him damp and unyielding, the humidity pressing it to his skin, not allowing it to escape him. Hick closed his eyes, but not for long. As soon as they were shut, nightmares loomed before them, and when they opened the nightmare that was his reality crushed him.

He went to the office earlier each day. The death of Birdie Lee Stanton pricked at him, like a thorn embedded in the fleshy part of his foot, too deep to remove and always painful—something too close to his consciousness to be ignored.

The town was shocked when the mother was identified. Wayne Murphy declared it to be a rape, and therefore, another unsolved crime. Iva Lee had been a willing participant, of that Hick was sure, but there was a question of statutory rape, and because of this, the man would not come forward.

Adam was certain Iva Lee had killed the baby, not on purpose, but maybe accidentally trying to clean the afterbirth off at the slough. It was plausible, Hick admitted, but Iva Lee's declaration that someone took the child put doubt into his mind. He didn't think she had the wherewithal to make up such a tale, or comprehend the need to lie about drowning the baby. Though Adam and Wash were ready to close the case, Hick was not.

As he sat at his desk, dully staring out the window, the door of the station opened and Fay stepped in, looking relieved to find Hick there at such an early hour.

"Hick, Tobe's real bad this time. He's been drinking all night."

Hick glanced at his watch. It was seven in the morning. "He got the gun out again?"

Fay nodded. "This is the worst I ever seen him. When I told him I thought he should put the gun up he looked at me real sad like and said, 'Fay, I want you to take Bobby and get to your mother's.'" She began to cry. "I'm afraid he's gonna do himself a harm."

Hick grabbed his hat and headed for the door. "Wait here for Wash or Adam and tell them where I've gone. Tell them to stay here. I want to talk to Tobe myself."

She nodded, but grabbed his arm as he walked passed her. "Please, Hick. Be careful."

He nodded and left the station, pausing to make sure Wayne Murphy was not watching. It was early and his office was still closed. At least there was that.

He raced to Tobe's house out on Ellen Isle, a small rural community with no post office, school, bank, or church. It had a few tenant farm houses, but no one knew where it had gotten its name or why it even had one.

The Hill household was down a deserted dirt road, beside which ran Lem Coleman's cotton fields. In the sunshine, the plants were blossoming, the recent rain helping them to grow tall and green. The ruts and grooves in the road were deep and Hick's car jolted painfully through them. He zigzagged, trying to escape the worst of them and finally spied the house in the distance.

It was an old tenant house, used by the pickers who would migrate down to the county from the hills that lay to the southwest. They came to these parts every October for the cotton and made enough money from picking to live on most of the next year. The tenant houses were not designed for comfort and were not ideal for year-round living, but it was all they could afford on Fay's meager salary.

The porch was rotten and caving in on one side and the steps were gone, replaced with a cinder block. Tobe sat sprawled on the edge of the porch with his feet on the block and his rifle across his lap.

Hick climbed from his car and approached slowly. He knew Tobe was unpredictable when drunk, and Fay had not understated his level of intoxication.

"Tobe, you know you're not supposed to be firing that

weapon. You're scaring the neighbors again."

Tobe wrapped his fingers around the barrel of the rifle, gently fondling the metal with his thumb. Hick remembered that motion, the long sweeping caress done with amazing fluidity for a thumb so rough from work. In high school, Tobe would hold a baseball behind his back before a pitch. It was as if he could see the ball through the pores and wrinkles and follicles of his skin. Hick admired this as he played shortstop behind his friend, but today, impeded by too much whiskey, it was doubtful Tobe understood the lethality of what he held in his hands.

Tobe looked up. He seemed confused as to how Hick got there. "I ain't fired it, yet," he protested with a slur.

"Fay came to the office and said you was about to. You scared her bad this time."

Tobe seemed to consider. "Where's she now?"

"Her mother's."

"Is she comin' back?"

Hick hated to see his friend reduced to this. Tobias Hill, the boy who was going to the majors, who everyone believed was the best of the best. During basic training he was warned to shoot poorly at the rifle range. Everyone told him what would happen, but Tobe was nothing if not competitive. His score earned him a place with the snipers and he lost count of the men he'd killed.

"She'll come back if you give me the gun."

The hand on the barrel clenched tighter, the thumb firmly pressed. "My gun?"

Hick raised his foot and rested it on the porch, leaning forward and looking into his friend's face. "Tobe, the war's over."

Tobe turned to Hick. His dark eyes were moist and he blinked quickly. "We both know it ain't ever over."

Their eyes met in mutual understanding. Hick held out his hand. "For Fay?"

Again, Tobe's thumb caressed the steel barrel. Hick thought Tobe could never touch a woman with as much tenderness and love as he was touching that gun.

"Is it the only way?" Tobe asked, with a little sob.

"They're after me to lock you up because of it. You need to give it to me."

For a split second, Tobe's eyes grew wide and fearful. They darted left and right, as if afraid some trick was being played. Then, he shuddered a little, as if trying to force his splintered mind back to reality. He rose unsteadily, and Hick took a quick step backward, thinking Tobe had been angered.

The drunken man stood there, helplessly, and then hesitantly raised his arm toward Hick, the butt of the rifle scraping the porch. Hick's hand wrapped around the barrel and in a swift motion, he pulled it to his chest, afraid Tobe might have a change of heart.

Tobe stood there, stunned, looking at his gun in Hick's hand. "I got a pistol, too," he finally managed. "I'd like to keep it if you don't mind. It ain't what I fire that gets everyone riled up. The army issued it to me."

"No one complained about a pistol," Hick said as he walked away from the porch carrying the rifle. He paused as he put it in the back seat of the car. Tobe was staring at him as if he were taking his wife away, not with anger, but with hurt and betrayal.

Hick came back to the porch. "Why do you do this, Tobe? Why are you hurting yourself and everyone around you like this?"

Tobe sat down hard on the porch, the weight of the man causing it to groan and mutter. He picked up the bottle of Jim Beam and took a swig, wiping his mouth on his sleeve. "Do you ever see them, Hick? Do you ever see the faces of the men you killed?"

"Yes."

"God, they were young."

"So were you. You were just obeying orders, Tobe. We all were."

Tobe took another long pull at the bottle and smiled drunkenly. "But that's where you're wrong, my friend. I wasn't just obeying orders … I enjoyed it." Thunder rolled far in the distance, the sound sweeping across the flat delta.

Hick folded himself onto the porch beside his friend. "What do you mean?"

"To me it was a kind of game. I'd tell myself I killed ten yesterday, let's go for twelve today. I enjoyed hearing, 'Good work, soldier'. I enjoyed the challenge."

"Tobe, you're a hero. Those men you killed could have killed one of our boys. You saved lives."

"By taking them?" He laughed. "You know when it finally hit me, what I'd done? I came home and there stood Fay with my little Bobby. Shit, I'd never seen him before, and there he was. He looked just like me, and then it hit me. I didn't just kill soldiers. I killed men like me—like you—men who were fathers or who would someday be fathers. I killed all the little Bobbys that would come after them. I killed them and their children in one fell swoop because it was a fun little game. Goddamitt, Hick! It was no game." He began to sob and Hick sat beside him stricken.

Tobe took a long drink and held the bottle up in front of his face. "This is the only thing that helps me forget. It helps me forget what I've done." His face dropped. "It helps me forget what I am, and one thing's for goddamn sure, I ain't no hero."

"Tobe, you did what you were expected to do. What'd you think you were going to do over there?"

Tobe laughed. "I didn't reckon on liking it."

"You weren't yourself over there. None of us were." A small flash of lightning sparked, followed by the low rumbling of thunder. Hick saw rain in the distance, dark streams of water quenching the dusty earth.

"Oh, I was myself alright," Tobe contradicted. "I was the big man. I always liked to be the big man. Best shot in the company. I've got a box full of medals congratulating me on the men I killed." He took a long swig. "I'd trade 'em all if I could bring just one of those boys back. Give just one of them the chance to have a Bobby of his own." He paused and smiled a crooked smile. "But I don't reckon that'll be happening, now will it?"

Hick shook his head and answered, "No, Tobe, they can't come back." He paused and then said, so quietly that at first Tobe couldn't hear him, "I killed a civilian."

"What?"

Hick reached for Tobe's bottle and drank deep. It burned all the way down and sat in his stomach burning and churning. "I killed an unarmed civilian. Hell of a soldier I was." He took another long drink, noting that the storm was going around them, close enough to feel the cool dampness, but not close enough to wet the parched earth.

Tobe took the bottle back from Hick and asked, "What happened?"

The whiskey was already going to Hick's head. The heat, the hunger, and the lack of sleep made his eyes feel heavy and his head light. He liked it and reached for another drink. "My company got hit pretty bad. There weren't many of us left and we were all split up. Hell, I hadn't been in Belgium a month. I didn't know how to fight … I didn't even have my bearings. None of us did. A bunch of green kids thrown out into an ice cold forest." He took another long drink, vaguely aware that it no longer burned going down.

"I followed my sergeant into an old farmhouse. It should have been deserted. Hell, it was in the middle of a battlefield. We went inside and I got jumpy. I saw a shadow move and called for it to 'Halt!' Instead it ran. What the hell was I supposed to think? I shot it."

Tobe nodded, drunkenly. "That's what we do in war, my friend. We shoot to kill and we ask questions later."

"Like you, I was a good shot. Right in the head. My God, I'd never seen so much blood. No weapon … too young to be a soldier." Hick snatched the bottle from Tobe swallowing a long drink. He handed the bottle back with shaking hands. He shook his head. "Not even a soldier." A small breeze blew up, cooling the sweat from Hick's forehead.

"A life is a life whether they're in uniform or not," Tobe reasoned.

Hick shrugged, his speech beginning to slur. "That's the face I see. I see it every day … a life wasted for nothing."

"It was all for nothing," Tobe contradicted, and then he began to laugh. "And here we sit, as good as dead ourselves. We sell our souls to Uncle Sam, and he gives us a flag-draped coffin and a free headstone."

Hick took another long drink from the bottle, realizing that for the first time in a long time, nothing hurt. The cool breeze from the storm and the lightness of his head were pleasant. He felt nothing but a mellow softness in his brain that made the war seem very far away. For an hour, he sat beside his friend sharing the whiskey until it was gone. The last thing he remembered was Tobe rising to get another bottle.

16

Hick woke in his bed with his head aching and the room spinning. He went straight to the bathroom, too sick to marvel at how he had gotten home. He lay on the floor moaning and cursing himself for being such a fool.

Vaguely, he recalled Adam's face over him, looking concerned, and he seemed to remember being driven home, although they must have stopped for him to be sick. It was all fuzzy, but details were beginning to come back. He remembered asking Adam to not say anything to Pam or his mother, and he remembered Fay's concerned look as Adam helped him into the squad car. After that, nothing. He couldn't recall how he got into the house or into bed. He glanced out the window and his car was in front. No one would know what he had done the day before except Tobe, Adam, and Fay, and yet shame overwhelmed him.

Sitting at the kitchen table, he put his head in his hands, the incessant pounding made opening his eyes painful. His watch read five o'clock. He needed to get ready for work, but every time he moved his stomach lurched and the room spun.

Finally, after a half an hour, he was able to lift his head and walk to the bathroom. He cut himself shaving, which he never did, and pulled on a shirt, slightly more rumpled than usual. With no time to make coffee, he would have to run into the diner. Black coffee was just what he needed to clear the dust and cobwebs from his brain.

The strong smells of eggs, pancakes, and bacon assailed his stomach when he lumbered through the doorway. Making his way to the counter, he sat down and covered his eyes with his hand, trying to shut out the bright light that poured in through the large picture windows.

Maggie appeared with a cup of black coffee. He didn't open his eyes, he didn't have to—her sweet perfume blended with strong coffee, and he knew it was her. Blindly, he reached for the coffee and put it to his lips, its bitterness making his stomach flop, but he forced it down and asked in a raspy voice for more.

When she reappeared, she put a glass in front of him. It didn't smell like coffee and he opened one eye. "What's this?"

"Drink it," she said, quietly.

He raised the glass to his lips and took a sip, then grimaced. "God, what is it? It's awful!" Painfully, he raised his eyes to her face.

"Tomato juice, a raw egg, and Tabasco. I know a hangover when I see one."

For once, he was too sick to blush.

"Drink it down," she told him, "it'll help."

He held his nose and drank, feeling his stomach heave with each swallow. He sat there, tortured by all the typical sounds that had never bothered him before. The clanking of silverware against dishes, the cheerful patter of the towns-folk, even the bell clanging against the door every time it opened. Everything caused his head to pound in agony. She came back with another cup of coffee. Again, he opened one eye and looked at her. "How do you know so much about hangovers?"

"You'd be surprised at how many of our 'respectable' cit-izens come in here looking just like you."

He forced a faint smile.

"What were you thinking? You've never been so asinine before."

"I went to get Tobe's gun."

"You tried to drink with Tobe Hill?"

"I didn't try. It just happened."

She shook her head. "How?"

"We started talking about the war and one thing led to another."

"You talked about the war?"

He nodded.

She tried to sound careless when she asked, "What did you say?"

He put the cup on the saucer and looked into her face. "I said I did some things over there that I can't seem to get past. Mistakes that can't ever be made right."

"Do you think ... " She hesitated and lifted the cup and

saucer wiping the counter beneath them. "Do you think you'll ever get past them?"

"I don't know. I'd be lying if I said I knew. I'm afraid if people … I … I'm afraid if you knew what I did, you'd hate me. I'd rather die than know that you're alive somewhere thinking less of me because of what I did."

"Order up, Maggie," called a voice from the kitchen.

She glanced behind her and then turned her attention back to Hick. "I could never hate you. There ain't nothing you could have done to make me hate you, because I know you'd never do anything wrong on purpose."

"You got orders here, Maggie!" the cook called again.

She left and took the food to a booth across the diner. When she returned, she had an intense look upon her face. "Hickory, when you came home and decided you needed to punish yourself, you punished me, too. Don't forget that. Don't ever forget that."

He pushed himself to his feet and turned away, pausing at the doorway to look back at her. Maggie was wiping a corner of her eye with her apron.

He walked across to the station and was met by Adam searching his face, trying to understand what had happened the day before. "I'm okay," Hick said, trying to reassure him. Proudly, he held up the rifle. "Wash, can you lock this away where Tobe Hill can't get it?"

"Hellfire," Wash said in admiration, "how'd you get it from him?"

Hick's eyes met Adam's. "We just talked about old times. That's all."

"How did the talking go?" Adam asked him.

Hick knew what he meant. "It went okay."

"And everything is okay today? I'm not going to have to go back out to Tobe's for any reason, am I?"

"No reason at all," Hick assured him.

Adam seemed satisfied.

Hick sat at his desk staring at the mound of paperwork. It needed to be done, yet his head ached and his stomach was queasy. The process of filling out forms took more fortitude than he seemed to have. The door to the station opened and he glanced up to see Fay coming in. He blushed, knowing she had seen him passed out and drunk on her porch but, after all, how many times had she found her husband in the same position?

She sat in the chair before his desk with a puzzled look on her face.

"How are you today, Fay?" he managed to ask, feeling uncomfortable and foolish.

Her purse was in her lap and she stared at her hands wrapped tightly around it. "Hick, I'm worried."

"Why?"

"It's Tobe."

Inwardly, he groaned. "Is he drinking?" He glanced at his watch. It was seven o'clock at night. There had been very few days that had found Tobe Hill still sober at that hour.

"No," she answered. "He took his bottles and dumped them in the yard and sat down at the table. He ain't moved, ain't ate nothing, ain't drank nothing. He's just sitting there."

"Did you speak to him?"

"I did. He just asked if I would mind taking Bobby and going to my mother's for a day or two. He said he's got some things he needs to work through." Her voice lowered. "He was looking at his pistol last night after Adam took you home."

Hick's heart stopped. Trying to sound calm he told her, "We was just talking about old times yesterday. Likely, he wanted to just look it over. I'll go on out there and make sure everything's okay."

She looked unsure. "Do you think it a good idea to go alone? Maybe you should take Wash or Adam."

Hick shook his head. "There's nothing wrong, Fay. You're worrying about nothing. Go on to your mother's. Things'll be fine."

She rose and paused uncertainly at the doorway. "Is there anything I can do?"

"Just go by Adam's and let him know. Tell him there won't be a repeat of yesterday."

She nodded and paused at the doorway. "It seems odd, really. It's been so long since he's been sober, I almost forgot what he was like."

"Things'll be fine."

She nodded and left and he watched her cross the street. With a pounding heart, he climbed into his car and sped out of town toward Ellen Isle. There could be only one reason for Tobe to be looking at that pistol, and Hick dreaded what he might find when he pulled up to the house. Tobe was not on the porch as usual.

Hick rushed up the porch and pounded on the door. "Tobe! Open up."

Relief flooded through him when the door opened and Tobe's face appeared on the other side. It was drawn and sickly. "Hey, Hick. How you feelin' today?"

Hick forced his way into the house and looked around. The pistol was in the middle of the kitchen table. "Is that loaded?"

"A gun ain't much good without ammo in it."

Hick sat down at the table and stared at it, wondering if he should grab it and go, or wait it out and see what Tobe had in mind.

Tobe sat heavily in the chair across from him. Scratching his eyebrow he said, "I forgot how lousy it is bein' sober." He looked terrible, the pain pouring from his body in the sweat that soaked his skin.

"I think you ought to give me the gun," Hick said in a soothing voice.

Tobe glanced up. "Why?"

"Because you're gonna feel worse before you feel better. I just think a loaded weapon is a dangerous thing to have in eyeshot."

"No," Tobe replied, "you took my shotgun. I want to keep the pistol … in case."

"In case what?"

"In case it gets too bad."

Hick leaned forward. "I can't let you keep it. I'm afraid you'll hurt yourself." Hick tried to put his hand over the pistol, but Tobe was larger and his long arms reached the gun first, his fingers wrapping around the pistol. Hick's hand closed over Tobe's, but Tobe wrenched backward, pulling Hick from his seat and sending the chair clattering across the floor. Tobe shook the gun, but Hick would not release his grip. Looking his friend in the eye, Hick said, "You need to let go. It's dangerous for you to have this in the shape you're in."

Tobe simply shook harder. "You done took one gun from me. I don't aim to give you another."

Tobe was a good three inches taller than Hick, so Hick found himself off balance trying to keep the gun within his grasp over his head. He gave one mighty tug, trying to loosen the weapon, but instead his hand slipped into Tobe's. The next thing Hick knew, there was a blinding flash and loud explosion, followed by a searing pain at the edge of his ear, and then he was on the floor, his back against the wall, his head throbbing.

"Oh, Jesus!" Tobe cried, flinging the gun away and rushing to Hick. He bent over his friend, his face colorless, his eyes round with disbelief. "Hick?"

Hick raised his head, dazed, the blast echoing in his ears. He put his hand on Tobe's shoulder. "Help me up."

As he sat up, the blood began to trickle down his neck. He could feel it cool and sticky against his skin. He felt woozy and sick when he rose.

"My God, Hick," Tobe said, in a shaky voice, "I don't know what happened."

"It was an accident," Hick managed through clenched teeth. "I bumped your hand. I know it was an accident."

Tobe helped him to a chair. "Let me get Doc," he said.

"No," Hick returned, quickly. "I don't want anyone to

know. Tobe they could put you away for this. You barely grazed me."

Tobe looked unconvinced. "Hick, there's a piece of your ear on my floor."

Hick looked into his friend's face. "Tobe, I want you to listen to me. I'm going to go home and tomorrow this will be over. I don't want you to say a word to anyone about what happened to me today. You hear?"

"Let me get the doc," Tobe begged.

Hick rose from the chair. "No, Tobe. I mean it. It looks worse than it is. You go to bed. You'll feel better in the morning."

Hick walked to his car, trying to stand up straight and walk as if nothing was wrong. The pain was intense, his ear throbbed and burned. The blood was soaking into his shirt staining it dark red. He glanced once more at Tobe's stricken face and managed to wave before he climbed inside.

He drove into town, intending to stop by the station and get the extra shirt he kept there. Getting out of the car, he noticed Maggie in the diner mopping the floor. Unsteadily, he headed across the street and stumbled inside to get some ice.

Maggie glanced up as he opened the door. In an instant, her face faded from copper to white.

"Hickory! My God, what happened to you? Sit down." She pulled up a chair and he gratefully sat down, feeling the blood flow down his neck.

"I just had a little accident. Do you have any towels?"

"Towels," Maggie repeated automatically and spun

around, grabbing one from behind the counter. She placed it to his ear and said, "Accident? What happened?" Her face was unnaturally pale; her lips were white and trembling, her eyes wide and fearful.

"It wasn't anything. Just a disagreement over a pistol between me and Tobe."

"Hickory, he could have killed you," she said, an edge of hysteria to her voice.

"It wasn't his fault. Please, don't tell anyone. It was just an accident." He gingerly felt his ear and winced in pain. "Do you have any ice?"

"Ice," she repeated and scurried into the kitchen. Suddenly, he heard a loud crash coming from the back of the café and he rose to see what had happened. Maggie was on the floor scooping up the little cubes of ice, and there were tears on her cheek. She looked up when he entered and said, "I'm sorry. I dropped it. I'll rinse it—"

"You don't have to rinse it," Hick told her. "I just need it wrapped in a towel. I'm not going to eat it."

She wrapped several cubes in a towel and rushed to him, placing it against his ear. He could feel her hand shaking and he reached up to get the towel and instead found his hand around Maggie's. Their eyes met and neither of them moved for what seemed to be a long while. His forehead met hers and they leaned together, he could hear her breath, it came in short, ragged sobs. His eyes were closed. He couldn't look at her face. He hadn't been this close to her since he returned to Cherokee Crossing, and he felt a sudden need to hold her. His hand tightened around hers and he swallowed hard.

"Mag, I want so much—"

The bell on the door startled them and Matt's voice was heard from the front of building calling, "Maggie? You here?"

Her hand instantly went down, the spell broken. "I'm back here," she called to him in a shaky voice.

Hick held the towel to his ear and walked to the front of the café greeting Matt with a handshake.

"Jesus, Hick," Matt exclaimed. "What happened to you?"

"Just a little work related accident," Hick told him, trying to sound casual. His shirt was soaked with blood, it was dried on the side of his head and he knew he looked worse than he really was.

Maggie emerged from the kitchen pale, but composed. "Hi, Matt," she said. Her hands were still shaking and Matt asked her, "You okay?"

She sat down. "I'm just not used to people showing up here with blood oozing out of them," she explained. "I'll be fine."

"I best get going," Hick told them. "Thanks, Mag."

Her pale lips formed the essence of a smile and he walked across to the station for the extra shirt.

17

Hick never realized that one could physically feel darkness. He didn't know that it could crush the air out of your lungs, that its fingers could tickle the back of your neck, that its whispers could cause you to hear voices that weren't there. He stood inside of the farmhouse, sweat rolling down his back in spite of the cold. Squinting into the blackness, he saw shadows, ghostly opaque images that flitted before his eyes.

Rigidly, he stood with his back against the wall, clutching his M1, pressing the wood of the gun to his chest. The core of his body shivered, his hands trembled, his breath came in shallow, stuttering gasps through chattering teeth. Everything in the house seemed to be alive, wriggling and squirming, as if the darkness itself was organic.

"Keep your eyes open," Sergeant Brody whispered. Hick jumped as a rhythmic, tapping noise became audible. He moved his finger to the trigger, his hands shaking, damp with sweat.

"Easy, Blackburn," whispered Sergeant Brody. "It's just snow melting off our gear."

The tapping was behind him, in front of him, all around him, and it continued as he clamped his hands around the gun, opening his eyes as wide as they would go, trying to see anything in the blackness. *Tap. Tap. Tap.* Hick turned his eyes to his sergeant, who motioned him to remain calm. *Tap. Tap. Tap.*

Hick sat up, gasping for breath and drenched in sweat, feeling the stifling heat of the house. The windows were closed against the rain that sprayed heavily against them. He reached for his ear. It throbbed and burned, the bleeding had stopped long ago, but it was swollen and bruised. He brushed a gnat away from it and swung his legs around, leaning his elbows on his knees and putting his head into his hands.

Again, he heard it … a patient tapping. He rose from bed, stumbling in the darkness and strained his hearing against the storm. He realized someone was knocking on the door, and he quickly pulled on some denim trousers and threw on his flannel shirt.

Blinking, he edged open the door to find Maggie standing there, dripping with rain. "Mag?" he said in surprise, quickly opening the door and letting her in out of the storm. "What are you doing here?"

She stepped into the dark house, and her eyes were on his face, studying it. "Are you alright? I've been worried sick all night, so I had to see you." She looked around and found the light switch.

She had never been in Hick's house, and he was embarrassed seeing it through her eyes. The dishes were piled in the sink and a roach scurried across the floor, fleeing the bright light. The ashtray on the table was running over and the newspapers he had taken from Wayne Murphy were scattered all over the kitchen chairs and table. He started to make an excuse but soon realized she didn't care.

"Let me get you a towel," he offered. He grabbed one from the linen closet down the hall and returned to the kitchen. She was standing at the sink filling the percolator with water. "Sit down and let me make you some coffee," she told him. She guided him to a chair and gently pushed him down, then took the towel and wiped the drops of rain from her face.

She cleaned the old coffee grounds out of the basket and refilled it. Then, she reached for the matchbox, lighting the stove as if she had always belonged there and put the coffee on. After moving some old newspapers, she sat down across from him.

"How's your ear? It looks like it hurts."

"I was gonna come see you this morning. It ain't that bad, really. It's just this little piece." He unwittingly touched it and winced at the pain.

"Will Tobe be okay?"

"I'm sure he'll be fine. He was sober when I left him. First time I seen him like that in years."

She nodded and absentmindedly folded a newspaper into little triangles.

There was an awkward pause and she looked around the

house for the first time. "So this is where you live now." Weakly, she added, "It's nice."

He scratched out a small laugh. "It's a wreck."

She shrugged her shoulders but smiled, and again began folding the newspaper.

Silence settled around them in the room, occasionally interrupted by a clap of thunder. The rain drummed against the tin roof and the smell of coffee perfumed the air. Hick fixed his eyes on the brown liquid as it spurted up into the glass dome. He glanced at the clock and watched the hand as it slowly inched forward, desperately trying to think of something to say.

"You scared me to death last night," she finally told him.

"I didn't know where else to go," he confessed. "When I saw you through the window ... I just needed to hear your voice." He hesitated and asked, "You didn't tell Matt what happened, did you?"

"I wasn't much in a talking mood."

Hick exhaled in relief. "He's a great guy. I know he'll make a good husband."

Maggie rose and walked to the stove, taking the percolator off the flame. "Yes, he'll make a wonderful husband." She turned back toward Hick. "He just won't be mine."

Hick's heart froze. "What?"

"I broke my engagement. I told Matt I couldn't marry him. Really, Hickory, it wouldn't be fair. I could never love him."

"Oh, Mag," Hick groaned, "Why did you do that?"

She turned away from him and opened a drawer, pulling

out two teaspoons. As she reached up to pull down the sugar bowl, her hand trembled. Finally, she sighed and looked down into the blue flame of the burner. "Hickory, for some strange reason, I can't seem to stop loving you. I have tried and tried, and I'm done trying. I'm a fool, no doubt, but there's some things I just can't help." She turned off the burner with an abrupt snap and her hand briefly wiped her cheek. Then she turned back to the table with a forced smile, bringing the sugar bowl and spoons.

Hick pushed back from the table and stood, motionless, arms hanging at his sides. In an instant, all of the letters she wrote him in Europe appeared before his eyes, all of the kisses, all the quiet moments, all the laughter, all their history. She was as much a part of him as his own self. A sob erupted from somewhere deep inside. "Oh, God," he moaned. His carefully built wall was giving way, the pain creeping in through the crevices.

She pulled some cups from the cabinet, peering inside of them, and said, "You don't have to feel bad. It ain't your fault, really."

He went to the window. Through the darkness he could see the rain falling in waves, slamming against the pane, breaking into gentle rivulets as it streamed down the glass. Thunder rolled across the delta, low and rumbling, causing the house to tremble. He pressed his forehead to the smooth glass as the sorrow swelled within him, causing his shoulders to shudder.

"Coffee's done," Maggie said. He turned and saw two cups of coffee on the table. They looked companionable sitting together. "Your cream is curdled," she added, closing the door to his icebox and facing him.

He stood, unmoving, and looked at her with pain-filled eyes. "I want it to be over with … but I don't know how to make it go away."

She crossed the room. "Talk to me, Hickory. Let me help you."

"No one can help me," he said in a dull voice.

She stood close to him and her hand picked up the loose end of his shirt. Looking down at it, she rubbed the soft flannel between her fingers. "Let me try. You could always talk to me before."

He ran his hand through his hair and shook his head. "I thought I was gonna make it, but then this baby came along."

"It must have been awful, seein' a baby like that."

He looked into her eyes. "It ain't the first time I seen a dead baby."

He saw her stiffen as if ready to receive a blow. Her face was composed. He knew she was waiting. The grief and sorrow that had consumed him, which had become a part of the very marrow of his bones, began to eke out. "I stood by and watched a little girl get killed in Belgium. I didn't lift a finger to help … I didn't stop it. I just watched." He waited, his eyes closed, for the sound of her leaving.

"What happened?" She was still there. Her voice was low and gentle, filled with so much love it made his whole body ache.

He squeezed his eyes shut, trying to blot everything out,

his face pinched, his forehead wrinkled. Pressing the bridge of his nose with his thumb and forefinger, he said in a stifled voice, "I killed somebody that shouldn't have been killed. A woman … a mother." He felt something cold and wet form in the corner of his eye and was vaguely aware that it was a tear. "I thought she was a Nazi … I couldn't see … I was scared. So I shot her." The room began to close in on him. He struggled to breathe, his head ached, and his throat was tight. "She stayed behind because it was so cold and she wanted to protect her baby. It was so tiny. Couldn't have been more than a few hours old. They were hiding out in a dark, abandoned house and were wrapped in quilts. It must have been terrifying for her when we ran in there. She jumped and I shot. And then, the baby … the baby started to cry, and my sergeant said we couldn't take it with us 'cause it'd give us away."

His head slumped forward and his shoulders shook. "The next thing I knew he'd killed the baby. Someone would have found her … I know they would have. I should have stopped him, but I didn't. I just stood there and watched him aim the pistol and pull the trigger."

"Oh, Hickory." Maggie's voice was soft and mournful in his ear, and he realized he was on his knees and she was there beside him. "What could you have done?"

"I could have stopped it, there had to be something I could do. But I didn't. I killed a woman and might as well have killed her child."

"You didn't kill a baby. A monster did that."

"No," Hick said, quickly, "Joe Brody was my friend. He

came and found me after I got the letter about my dad. He took me under his wing, like a big brother. I owe him my life." He could feel her hands in his hair, smoothing it, gripping it, and desperately trying to grasp what was happening inside of him. Her face was near his, her breath soft on his cheek.

"I watched Joe aim that pistol and shoot that baby like it was a rat. I respected him; I still do. But I don't understand how he could do that ... with no remorse. He just kind of shrugged and said it was nothing but a damned kraut anyway. But, he's no monster. I knew him as well as I know Adam or Wash."

"But they would never do anything like that."

"You don't know that, Mag. People are like animals when their survival is threatened."

"I can't believe that," she answered him. "Would you have done that? Could you have killed that child?"

He shook his head. "I don't think so, but I don't trust myself anymore. I can't find that one shred of decency in me that might convince me I wouldn't. If someone were to tell me I'd stand aside and watch a baby murdered, I'd have never believed it."

"Oh my God," Maggie said, tearfully "you were eighteen-years-old. It was a war. People die in wars."

"Not me. I didn't die there ... I just die here in little pieces, a little more each day."

Her hands were on his face, pulling him toward her. She kissed his forehead, his eyes, and her lips moved across his cheek to his ear. "Hickory, there's more to you than what you did there. You can't stop living because of one mistake. You are more than that one moment."

"Am I?"

"It was an accident. It was war. It's not fair to blame yourself."

"Maybe not. But it doesn't change what happened. I can never bring her back. My God, she was young. I see her face every night when I close my eyes. I replay what happened over and over in my head, wondering what I could have done, what I could have changed. If I hadn't been so jumpy, if I had waited before I shot."

"But you didn't know it was a woman."

He sighed heavily. "Would it have made a difference?"

"Yes. You wouldn't have shot. But you didn't know, and you can't let that haunt you the rest of your life."

His head drooped and a solitary tear splashed onto the floor.

Maggie's hand rested on his cheek. "You can't bring her back. You can't change what happened."

He glanced up at her, afraid to see the disappointment on her face. It was tear-stained and red, her hair tucked behind her ears, hanging in wisps around her neck, her eyes full of love and pain and sorrow. "I thought it was over," he said, "but then this baby came along. I don't know what happened to it, and I'm afraid to find out because as far as I know, it could be anyone."

Her hands moved down his neck to his shoulders and she looked into his eyes. "You'll find out what happened, and I promise you the sun will still rise the next day."

He had told no one what he had done, what he had seen. It was as if his heart remembered how to beat, it physically jarred in his chest as if a weight had been released. They were on the floor, kneeling together, and he pulled her close, conscious of the very breath in her lungs, the blood flowing through her veins, unwilling to let her go. Pain that had settled in his soul, erupted from him in painful, convulsive gasps.

He kissed her cheek and her hair, resting his mouth near her ear, breathing in her smell. "When I came home from basic, my dad told me I was gonna see a lot of bad things. He said he couldn't protect me anymore." Hick shook his head. "I needed to talk to him when I got back, and he was gone. I knew he was dead, but I could still see him. I'd walk into a room and think he was there, or I'd go out to the shed and open the door and smell his aftershave. For a while I thought I was going crazy. I had to get out of that house because he was everywhere, not alive, but not dead either." He paused. "And I'm just like him. I can't even remember what it feels like to be alive."

She put her lips on his. They filled him with longing, and he wrapped his arms around her tightly. "We can get through this," she whispered as his lips traveled down to her neck. "I promise, we'll get through this."

"I didn't want to love you. I tried to stop because I wanted you to have better."

She shook her head in protest, unable to speak.

He pushed her back, looking into her face, his thumb gently gliding across her cheek. "You don't know how many times I thought about you, wondering if we could start over again."

"You should have said something. You had to know I was waiting."

He took her hand and looked down at it. "I don't know why you would wait, why you would still want me."

"I've wanted you since the day your sister wheeled you over in that little Radio Flyer wagon you used to have."

He smiled, still looking at her hand. "I remember. You were under the house pulling out some kittens a mama cat had abandoned. My God, you were filthy."

"And you looked like a little prince being pulled around."

His face was troubled. "I'm not the same person I was. I don't know if I'll ever be the same."

"People change. I'm not the same either. It wears on a soul, wondering day in and day out if it's finally time to just give up the fight. It hurts to watch someone you love suffering and not being able to help."

He shook his head. "I've put you through hell."

"You've put us through hell. There was never a you and me … it's always been us."

"Do you trust me enough to try again?" he asked her.

She looked directly into his eyes. "I trust you with my life, Hickory. I always have."

He took a deep breath, then took her hands and kissed each palm. He urged her to her feet while he remained kneeling on the floor.

"Marry me?" he asked looking up into her face.

He heard her breath catch. "You've asked me that before."

"Will you?"

"When?"

"We can drive to the court house for the license tomorrow."

"And, then?"

He looked at her strangely. "Are you bargaining with me?"

She smiled, her old teasing smile. "I've got a lot of work to do if I'm going to live in this pig sty."

He rose. "Three days?"

She glanced around her. Holding out her hand to shake his, she answered, "It's a deal."

He brushed her hand aside and sealed the bargain with a kiss.

18

Hick glanced out the window of the bathroom. The storm clouds scurried away, the blue sky peeking out in pockets between them. He put on his tie and found Maggie in the kitchen finishing up the dishes. For the first time since Sheriff Michaels hired him, he was going to be late. Pulling his hat far down over his eyes, he asked Maggie, "Does it show?"

She crossed the room and peered at his ear. "Yes. Even if you could get all the dried blood off, it would still be twice as big as the other one."

"Damn," he muttered.

"There's no hiding it. It's black and blue." She reached up and shifted his hat back a little. "There's a little piece gone, too." She sighed. "He could have easily killed you, you know."

"I know that," Hick replied. "But he didn't."

"Poor Tobe. Who would have thought he'd turn out this way?"

"I haven't given up on him yet," Hick answered.

"You're probably the only one in town who hasn't."

"I've never known Tobe to fail at anything when he put his mind to it."

"True," Maggie agreed. "God, you two were always so cocky, walking around town like you owned the place."

He looked at her for a moment. "We were, weren't we?" he admitted. "I thought I had everything figured out. It's amazing how wrong a man can be."

She slid to him and put her arms around his waist. "Wrong about everything?"

"Not everything," he replied, kissing her forehead. He glanced at his watch. "I'm going to be late." He pulled his hat back down and shrugged. "Hopefully, Adam will just let it alone when I tell him it was an accident."

Maggie reached up, straightening his tie. "I wouldn't count on it. He's never left anything alone before."

They drove into town together and Hick parked in front of the diner. Glancing at the newspaper office, he saw Bill Stanton's car out front. "I don't like the look of this."

He left Maggie and hurried to the newspaper office, jerked the door open, and was greeted with the sight of Bill Stanton's shotgun aimed at Wayne Murphy's head.

"What in the hell is going on here?" Hick demanded.

Bill glanced at Hick without moving. "This son of a bitch interviewed my Iva Lee. It's in the paper and I want to know when he was slinkin' around and what exactly he done."

Wayne Murphy quivered, his hands in the air, his face pale. "I just talked to her, Bill. I done told you."

"Here's the problem," Hick told Murphy. "First, you were told to stay away from Iva Lee and you didn't, so you got no respect for the law. Second, you told me yourself that the truth ain't something you regard highly, so I can't believe you."

Murphy shifted his eyes away from Bill Stanton for a brief second. "Are you accusing me of something, Sheriff?"

"I'm sayin' there's enough evidence to put you at the top of my list of suspects."

"You can't be serious."

"Why not?"

"Why? Because I'm a well-respected person in this community. A business owner."

"In Cherokee Crossing a man is only as good as his word. It don't seem your word is worth much. I believe you agreed to leave Iva Lee alone, didn't you?"

"I did. But Bill and Rose were so stubborn. They wouldn't bring her to me, even though I asked."

"And your right to print a story is stronger than their choice to keep you from their daughter? Is that right?"

"There's a little thing called freedom of the press," Wayne argued.

Bill Stanton cocked the gun, its aim never moving. Murphy glanced at him, uneasily. "Well, ain't there?"

"You've gone beyond any freedom of the press. I'm afraid I'm gonna have to arrest you."

"Arrest me?" Murphy cried. "On what charge?"

"Well, let me see," Hick began. "We can start with tampering with a witness and possibly go all the way to obstruction of justice. We can certainly charge you with trespassing, and we might end up charging you with statutory rape … just to name a few."

Murphy's face was red with anger. "You can't do this."

Hick glanced at Bill Stanton. "It might be jail is the best place for you … for now, anyway."

Murphy's lips trembled a little and he seemed to think it over. "I'll go, but you got nothin' on me."

"Well, that'll be for the judge to decide," Hick replied. "Let me see the paper."

Stanton's gun remained fixed on Murphy's head. Without flinching, he tossed the newspaper to Hick.

This reporter was able to sit down with Iva Lee Stanton, the mother of the baby found in the slough last month. She described the child's father as a loving, generous man and is anxious to find him. In my humble opinion, the miscreant will not return to her. Perhaps on one of her evening soirées, she will find him, and the two lovers will finally be re-united.

Hick quietly sat the paper on the counter and his anger built inside him. He ran his hand over his eyes. His head grew warm and his heart pounded. Without warning, he rounded the counter, and before he consciously realized what he was doing, he seized Wayne Murphy by the collar and shoved him, hard. The noise of Murphy's head banging against the wall brought Hick back to his senses. Murphy was staring at him in shock, his face white.

"This man ain't nobody's lover, Murphy. He's a rapist, someone who belongs behind bars. He took something innocent and crushed it. It ain't nothing to make light of."

"I ... I ... wasn't making light—"

"You were. You used her just like he did." Hick narrowed his eyes, a glint of anger flashing. "You're no better than him."

"You think you're so high and mighty," Murphy returned, "with all your ideals and notions of right and wrong. What are you but the sheriff of a two-bit town? What do you know about anything?"

"I'll grant I ain't got the book learning you've got, but my daddy taught me something about compassion and understanding."

Murphy smirked. "Compassion and understanding doesn't sell papers."

"Maybe. But when I'm dead and gone, people will remember it. What will they remember about you?"

Bill Stanton's hand went to the trigger of his shotgun. "Why don't we find out right now?"

Hick's voice was low, but full of gravity. Still grasping Murphy by the collar, he said, "Don't do it, Bill. You'll spend the rest of your life regretting it."

Bill remained still, his finger on the trigger. He stared at Murphy, as if imagining the bullet going into his skull. After another moment, he uncocked the gun. "Murphy, you're nothin' but a heartless bastard." His voice broke. "My baby's had a rough time of it since her brain got hurt. The missus and me are doing the best we can, but it ain't been easy." He composed his emotions but added, "You remember this ... if you ever come around talkin' to her again, there ain't no jail will keep me from you. By God, I'll skin you and hang you out to dry. You got that?"

Sweat glistened on Murphy's forehead. He licked his lips and after a moment's hesitation, nodded.

Wash and Adam looked surprised when the three men entered the station. "What have we got here?" Wash asked.

"I'm arresting Wayne Murphy for trespassing," Hick answered. "Might be more charges coming."

"Don't be ridiculous" Murphy spat. "There'll be no more charges."

"We'll just see about that," Hick replied. He guided Murphy to the cell and locked the door behind him. Turning to Bill Stanton, he said, "I'm sorry about all of this, Bill."

Bill's gun rested at his side, the butt of his rifle on the floor. "You got any ideas on the daddy yet?" He turned angry eyes toward Murphy. "I still got my money on this weasel."

"We're workin' on it," Hick assured him.

"You keep me informed." With one last glance at Murphy, Bill Stanton left the station.

Hick went to the cell. "How long were you with her, Murphy?"

"Not more than a half-hour."

"Where'd you meet?"

"I saw her out walking down the road, so I picked her up. I wasn't on Stanton property so you can't get me for trespassing."

"Is that the first time you picked Iva Lee up?"

Murphy narrowed his eyes. "What are you driving at?"

"I'm just wondering if you've been alone with her before."

"No. It was like pulling teeth to get the girl to even make sense."

Adam joined them. "Murphy, what are we supposed to do with you? We explicitly told you to leave her alone."

"But I saw her walking. What was I supposed to do … not ask her?"

"In a word, yes," Adam replied. "You know you done gone and got yourself put on a pretty short list of suspects here. We could be talkin' murder, Wayne. It ain't nothing to trifle with."

Wayne sat down on the cot at the end of the room with his head in his hands. "I didn't do anything," he protested.

Hick shook his head, went to his desk and absentmindedly took off his hat. He pulled out some forms and Adam followed him. He sat down on the side of Hick's desk, and said, "You look like you got hit by a truck, boy. Want to talk about it?"

Hick's hand went up to his ear. "Just an accident."

"Doc see it?"

"It's fine," Hick answered. "What's left will heal and what's gone ain't comin' back."

"Doc could—"

"I said its fine," Hick interrupted with the note of finality in his voice that most people recognized.

Adam seemed to be pondering if he should pursue the issue. Evidently, he decided against it because, instead he asked the usual, "Where'd you eat breakfast?"

Hick cleared his throat. "Uh … Maggie made my breakfast." He quickly looked back down at his paperwork, feeling the familiar blush cross his face.

Adam's eyebrows rose. "I see." After a pause, he asked, "And how does Matt feel about that?"

"She broke it off with him."

"And?"

Hick looked up from the paperwork. "I'm gonna need a little time off in the next few days. I'm getting married at the end of the week."

Adam stared for a moment. "It's about damned time," he muttered, walking back to his desk.

The door opened with a groan, and Lem Coleman entered the station, his massive, thick frame filling it. Crossing to Hick's desk, he said, "Morning, Sheriff." He sat a pistol on it.

Hick looked up in surprise. "What's this?"

"Tobe Hill come by to see me this morning looking for work, sober as a judge. I put him right out in the fields choppin' cotton. Anyway, he asked if I would bring this to you and have you lock it up."

Hick stared at the pistol and then told Lem, "I'm obliged to you for bringing it in. I got the shotgun, but he didn't want to part with this."

"Sheriff, if you don't mind me sayin', I'm grateful. You done took a weight off the wife's mind. She says she don't know how you did it, but you must be some kind of magic man to have finally talked some sense into Tobe Hill."

The words "magic man" grabbed Hick's attention.

"I'm not magic," he protested, "it's all on Tobe, whether he can keep himself straightened out."

"Well," Lem answered, "he's a good worker, and I'm proud to have him."

Hick looked into Lem's honest face. It was burned red from hours of hard work in the sun. As teenagers, Tobe and Hick would laugh at Lem and the other farmers for their red skin, dirty hands, and backward ways. He understood so little about the world back then. He rose and shook Lem's hand. "Thanks for giving him a chance."

Lem nodded and headed across the street to the diner and Hick's eyes followed him. Shoving aside the paperwork, he said to Adam, "If you boys don't mind, I'm gonna take an early lunch. I got a good-lookin' gal across the way I want to visit with."

He walked to the door and Murphy called, "What about me? How long you gonna keep me here?"

"Got to talk to the judge first, and it's the Fourth of July. I'll try to reach him tomorrow."

Murphy's eyes widened. "You're tellin' me I might have to spend the night here?"

"No, Wayne. I'm tellin' you that you *are* spending the night here." Murphy's shout of protest followed.

Hick entered the diner and went straight to the counter.

"What can I get for you, Hickory?" Maggie asked like she did most days. Today, it seemed to mean so much more. He couldn't see enough of her. His eyes followed her every movement: the way she walked, the way she poured coffee, the way she smiled. Her laughter came to him from every corner of the diner. She was sparkling, her face bright and happy, her movements light.

He followed her back to the kitchen where she had gone to refill the iced tea pitcher. He grabbed her around the waist and pulled her close. He kissed her, unwilling to let her go.

You're gonna get me in trouble," she whispered, smiling. "Customers aren't supposed to be back here."

"Sheriff's business," he murmured, kissing her again.

"I have to get back," she whispered in his ear.

"I'll pick you up after work," he said. "I need to talk to your mama."

She playfully shined his badge. "What have you got to do today, Sheriff Blackburn?"

"This and that. Nothing urgent. I think, right now, I'll just go for a walk."

She kissed him again. "See you at seven?"

"Six-thirty," he answered.

She laughed. "Get going."

With one parting kiss, he exited the diner and walked into the hot July sunshine. It was another muggy day, steam rising from the ground like from a hot kettle. He paused on the sidewalk, lighting a cigarette, and walked through the thick air, squinting against the bright morning sunshine. Heat shimmered from the cars and off the tin roof of the feed store. Dogs lay panting in the shade.

He stepped off the sidewalk and bypassed a puddle, then jogged across the street, following the sound of children shouting. In the city park, a stage had been set up at one end and people hurried about, setting up tables and chairs.

He stood and surveyed the scene with satisfaction. Though he had changed in the past few years, this was his town, where he'd grown up. For an instant, he remembered how it felt to belong. He tossed the cigarette to the ground and crushed it.

At the other side of the park, on the ball diamond, it seemed every little boy in Cherokee Crossing had congregated. Benji played shortstop behind Jack Thompson, much like Hick had played behind Tobe. He wondered if their lives would be interrupted by war. He walked over to an old maple tree that had been in the park for years. It had been stuck by lightning twice and yet green branches still flourished, growing up out of the trunk at odd angles. Floyd Thompson, Jack's little brother, sat on a branch watching the game. Hick approached him. "Hey, Floyd."

The little boy looked up, his face tear-stained. "Howdy, Sheriff."

"You okay?"

Floyd looked down. "Yes sir. I just hurt my hand."

Hick knelt before him. "Want me to take a look at it?"

He shook his head. "Henry ran home to get some iodine. It'll be okay."

"What'd you do?"

"Got a splinter off that old bat."

Hick rose and stretched his arms out, then said with false bravado, "You might not know this, but I am one of the best splinter removers in the county."

Floyd looked down at his hand. "Granny digs and digs with the needle." He seemed to be thinking. Finally, he held out his hand, fingers curled tight. "I'd be obliged if you'd take a look at it."

Hick sat beside him on the tree, and pulled out his pocketknife. "The trick is to cut the skin just a tiny bit above the splinter and then catch hold of it." As Hick spoke, he gently maneuvered his knife, distracting the boy by talking about the game. "All done," he told Floyd.

Floyd stared at his hand in disbelief. "You done a fine job, Sheriff."

Henry ran up at that moment, carrying a bottle of iodine. "Does your mama know you got that?" Hick asked, skeptical that Pam would let him take it from the house.

"No, Uncle Hick," Henry replied.

"Give it to me," Hick told him. "This stuff stings like the dickens if you wipe it in your eye." He took the bottle from Henry and opened it to paint the wound on Floyd's hand. As he did this, his eyes landed on Floyd's now outstretched fingers. Though not prominent, the skin between the third and fourth finger was webbed. A horrible feeling crawled down Hick's spine.

Clearing his throat, he said, "Floyd, you got some fancy lookin' fingers there."

"It's a sight, I know," Floyd agreed.

"I reckon a man could live his whole life and never see another set of fingers like that," Hick ventured, trying to force his voice to sound careless.

"No sir," Floyd replied. "My daddy's fingers were just the same."

Hick's breath caught in his lungs and his heart stopped

beating. A hollow feeling dropped into the pit of his stomach. He felt tears smart behind his eyes and he pulled his hat low over them. In a quiet voice, he said, "I reckon you miss your daddy a lot."

"Yes, sir," Floyd answered not taking his eyes from the iodine stain and blowing on the wound.

Hick put his arm around the child's shoulder. "You know I miss my daddy, too."

Floyd looked into Hick's face. "But you're a grown man."

"That don't matter none. When you love someone you miss 'em when they're gone. It don't matter how old you are, and it don't matter what they done." He rose. "Well, I got a little work to do." He paused and patted the boy's shoulder. "You take care."

He walked away from the park, his lighthearted mood gone. Everything was dark and closing in. He felt sick, his heart beating so hard it hurt, his hands cold and damp. He went to the station and Wash and Adam were gone. Turning to Murphy, he asked, "You know where Adam or Wash went?"

"They didn't say," Wayne returned coldly, unwilling to look at Hick.

Hick scribbled a quick note saying he was heading out to the Thompson's and then got into his car. Removing his hat, he ran his fingers through his hair. He stared at the steering wheel, unable to concentrate on anything for the feeling of shock and disgust coursing through his body. He knew what this could mean. It was likely that before he died, Ross Thompson had fathered a child with Iva Lee Stanton. Hick finally started the car. He needed to look in Ross's truck.

19

Hick had little recollection of Ross. He'd gone to high school with Adam, but in Hick's memory, he was just another sunburned, hard-working farmer. Of course, the Thompsons were highly respected in town. They were frugal and stoic, never ones to crave comfort. It was a well-known fact that Claire Thompson didn't believe in doctors. After Ross's birth, she had six increasingly difficult labors producing six sickly children that lived only days. When Jake Prescott tried to persuade her to let him assist with her labor her response was always the same: pain in childbirth was God's curse, and she would take her punishment without a doctor's help.

In the case of Ross's wife, the final labor took both mother and child. Hick was at home from Basic Training when this happened and he remembered that Jake was enraged. "It could have been prevented," he repeated over and over again.

Hick leaned forward, his chin near the steering wheel, trying to will the car to move faster. "How am I going to tell Claire?" was his first thought, and then it occurred to him that perhaps it would be best if he didn't. She had been through so much in her life, outliving her husband and children. Why add to her pain?

The truck stood in the yard, its presence there now seemed foreboding. He approached it and paused with his hand on the door handle, not sure of what he was looking for and afraid of what he might find.

Finally, he flung open the door. Steam smacked him in the face and a hot, strong smell of mildew filled the air with dank sweetness. He climbed in, and the humidity clung to him, wrapping itself around his body. His shirt stuck to his underarms, his chest heaved trying to breathe the hot, soggy air.

He glanced underneath the seat. The car was filled with sand and dried, caked mud. Mold grew along the bottoms of the doors, and dried grass and leaves hung from the brake pedal and clutch. He maneuvered around the steering wheel, lay across the seat, and opened the glove box. It was filled with sand and gravel, thick and hard, coming off in chunks beneath his finger. Beneath that, there were a few papers, molded and unreadable.

He looked on the floor of the passenger side. Besides an empty soda bottle, there was gravel and sand littered about, left behind from the water that had seeped in from under the floorboard. He grabbed the bottle and sat up when something caught his eye. Lying across the seat, he reached beneath it, pulling out a hair ribbon. It was mud-stained and already rotting, but little hints of pink showed through the grime. Claire had never worn such a ribbon.

He felt guilty holding it, as if some long dead secret had been dug up that should have stayed buried. He closed his eyes and gripped the hair ribbon. In his mind, he recalled Ross at his wife's funeral, a miserable, heartbroken man left with two small boys and an uneasy guilt because he wouldn't get the doctor. "That boy is devastated," Hick's father said after the funeral. "If it weren't for his mother, he'd have to farm those kids out." How had that heartbroken man sunk so low as to sleep with Iva Lee?

He crawled out of the truck, even the stifling heat of July seemed cool by comparison. He took off his hat and ran his sleeve over his eyes to dry the sweat that was burning them. He put his hat back on and turned, running straight into Claire.

"Miss Thompson! You scared the bejesus out of me."

"Is there something I can help you with, Sheriff?" she asked.

"No, ma'am. I was just finishing up some paperwork. That's all."

"About Ross?"

"Yes, ma'am.

She seemed to be scrutinizing him and he felt uncomfortable. "And what did you find?"

"Nothing new. I just needed to go through the truck once more."

"What's in your hands?"

He glanced down at the hair ribbon and soda bottle. He clasped the ribbon in his fist and thrust it into his pocket. "Nothing really." He held up the bottle. "Just a few odds and ends. The truck is pretty much empty. You plannin' on sending it to the dump any time soon?"

"Perhaps," she replied. "You're awful jumpy. Is something the matter?"

The ribbon felt heavy in his pant's pocket. He wanted to hide the truth from her if he could. "No. Everything's fine."

She glanced at the bottle. "What are you doing with that?"

"I was just cleaning the car out." He shrugged his shoulders. "You can return it for the deposit if you want."

"I would like the bottle," Claire told him. He handed it to her and, after a pause, she said, "Hick, be honest. What else did you find?" She held out her hand, and with a feeling of resignation, he reached into his pocket and handed her the hair ribbon. He expected her to appear confused, but instead she just looked at it and shook her head. "A little hair ribbon."

Feeling curious, Hick asked, "Ma'am, this might seem an odd question, but can you tell me what Ross's frame of mind was on the day of his accident."

"Why, what do you mean?"

He tried to sound nonchalant when he replied, "Oh, you know. Was he upset about something? Depressed maybe? Angry?"

Her face grew pale. "Hick Blackburn, what are you implying?"

"I'm not implying anything. It's my job to ask questions."

Her eyes shifted. She raised her hand to smooth the hair that was pulled back. Hick noticed the knuckles on her hand were arthritic, severely so, and he recalled Iva Lee mentioning "bulby" hands. A wave of realization swept over him, stealing his breath and making his heart skip. The revelation that Claire Thompson could be the murderer of the baby in the slough washed over him. His knees almost buckled.

"Is there anything the matter?"

"No, ma'am. I just need to get back to the station, that's all." He desperately needed to speak with Adam. He screwed up one investigation by not waiting for Wash and Adam to give their input. He would not make that mistake again. Not on something this important.

"You look pale. Come inside and have a glass of iced tea."

"No, thank you," Hick replied, turning to leave.

"Please, Sheriff," Claire begged, "just for a minute. You look peaked. Sit down and cool off. I know it was hot in that truck."

He turned to her. The pleading in her eyes made him feel sorry for her, and suddenly he doubted his instincts. He felt foolish. "A glass of tea would be nice. Thank you."

He followed her up the steps and into the house, sitting down in the front room while Claire went to the kitchen. "I saw the boys in town playing baseball," he called to her.

She joined him with the iced tea in her hand. "I expect most everyone's in town today for the Fourth of July."

"Yes, ma'am," he replied, taking the glass from her and drinking down a large gulp of tea.

"Is your tea okay?"

"Yes, ma'am. It's just what I needed. I appreciate you going to the trouble."

She smiled. "No trouble at all."

He finished and she rose and took the glass back to the kitchen. He waited politely for her return. After about five minutes she came back. "Sorry I was gone so long. It generally takes about five minutes."

"What?"

"Chloral hydrate. The dose you just took generally takes about five minutes to work."

He rose from the chair and felt suddenly dizzy; the room was spinning beneath him. He wanted to speak, but his speech slurred. Glancing at Claire's face, he felt suddenly impressed with how hard it looked. Everyone knew her life had not been an easy one. She worked like a dog for everything she had, but the face that stared at him was harsh, it seemed to be waiting for something.

"Don't look at me that way, Hick. I feel bad enough about this as it is. You know I can't let you tell anyone what you know."

He tried to walk to the door but fell, crashing hard onto the floor. His eyes questioned her, and Claire seemed to understand. She stood over him. "That son of mine," she said shaking her head. "I know a man has his needs, I didn't expect him to stay home and be a monk. But he was going to marry her. My son, Ross Thompson, going to marry an imbecile! What do you think I should have done ... sit back and let him make a laughing stock out of the whole family? By God, I wasn't about to let that happen."

Hick lay on his stomach. He could hear her words, and most of what she said registered in his mind. His body was limp He couldn't move a muscle, he couldn't feel anything, he couldn't speak.

"You were a good son to your daddy right up to the last. You would've never done him the way Ross did me. I'm sorry to have to do this." Those were the last words he heard, and then everything went dark.

20

The young woman's eyes were open, but lifeless. Outside, the wind raged against the old farmhouse, ice skittered against its clapboard frame. Hick's breath came in frosty gasps. "We've got to get out of here," he told Sergeant Brody, his voice shaking.

Brody looked out into the storm. "Not yet. A few more hours and the storm will blow over. Then we can make our way back."

Hick's head quivered uncontrollably. "No. We need to leave here now."

Sergeant Brody turned to him. He glanced at the young woman on the floor, her face frozen in death. He crossed the room to where Hick was kneeling, looking into her face, unable to move. Placing his hand on Hick's shoulder, he told him, "This is what war is. She's a casualty ... there are plenty more casualties out there. A lot of our boys are lying dead in the snow looking just like her. They didn't volunteer for this either. It's just the way it is."

Hick's eyes turned up to Brody, questioning.

Joe Brody shook his head. "You'll never be able to make sense out of a senseless act. This whole damn war is senseless, but we have to win. If you don't fight, you get exterminated. Just remember, Blackburn, the winners decide who lives and who dies."

Suddenly, Hick felt the burning friction on his face as he was being dragged across the room and toward the door. There was a feeling of dampness, which somewhere in his consciousness registered as blood. His eyes opened and he looked up into Claire Thompson's face. It was red from exertion and she stopped and straightened out, breathing heavily. He must have blacked out again, because the next time his eyes opened he found himself alone, his feet out the door and on the porch. Then, the sound of his squad car being started made him desperately try to remember what he was doing and where he was. The last thing he recalled was being rolled across the Thompson front porch and into the trunk of his car.

He must have dozed, because the silence after the storm woke him. Joe Brody had covered the mother and her child with a blanket. He was carrying a can of gasoline and meticulously pouring it over them.

"What are you doing?" Hick asked.

"A war crime tribunal is … unpleasant." Joe spread the gasoline throughout the room. They stood outside and watched as the roof finally caved in, the heat from the flames licking Hick's face, filling his nostrils with smoke.

Hick woke to that same strong smell. Groggily, he felt

the biting metal on his handcuffed hands and strained his eyes against the darkness. His legs were thrown over a spare tire and he soon realized he was in the trunk of his car. A strong smell of smoke and intense heat warned him of a danger he was unable to see. He drunkenly jerked at the handcuffs. The chain held tight and he jerked again, harder. The effort only produced two cuts on the tops of his wrists. He shook his head and tried to clear the fog from his mind. He felt sick and disoriented and his eyes would close regardless of the danger he was in.

The gun was heavy and cold in his hand. He caressed it, his finger playing around the trigger, drunk with the knowledge of the power it wielded. Pain and sorrow, the hurt that washed around him and then swallowed him could be ended today, now. At night when his buddies in the tent would sleep, Hick would take the pistol and press it to his temple, wondering if he could go through with it, wondering how much more pain it would take to give him the courage to pull the trigger.

He held the gun to his right temple, the steel digging into his skin, leaving a pock as he twisted it back and forth, his heart pounding, trying to will his finger to pull the trigger. An explosion made him jump.

A tire had exploded from the heat. The heat and smoke began to intensify. Soon, they would incinerate everything: Hick, the car, the handcuffs leaving nothing behind but the impression that a terrible accident had taken place. He kicked at the lid of the trunk and again, strained against the cuffs.

He shook his head and tried to comprehend where he was, but he was dizzy, disoriented, immobilized. He wanted to understand what was happening, his survival instinct screamed out for him to fight, but he was sick and dazed.

The inside of the trunk was unbearable, the sweat poured from him as if he was melting. His skin was hot, red and flushed, the heat dried out his mouth and eyes. He struggled for air. The black smoke suffocated him and filled his nostrils and burned his eyes. He shouted and kicked at the trunk again and again, hoping someone might hear him. But no one did.

Sweat dripped into his eyes, and he rubbed his face against his shoulder. The fire roared in his ears. He gave one last tug, crying out in pain as the cuffs dug deeply into his wrists. He was exhausted, unable to breathe or see as the fire grew stronger. Hick grew weaker. He closed his eyes and laid his head back. He took in deep breaths of smoke, knowing what it meant to burn to death and preferring smoke inhalation. As Maggie's face loomed up in his imagination, he began to feel himself drifting away.

Then a whoosh of cold air filled the trunk and jarred Hick to his senses. He felt someone's hands reach around him. He blinked against the brightness of the flames and tried to see who was there. Fingers groped for him. Strong hands clasped his shoulders, dragging him roughly from the trunk. The handcuffs were red hot and through his smoke-filled eyes he saw a shadowy figure splash a bucket of water toward him. The coolness washed over him, and everything faded as he felt himself dragged away from the heat.

The nausea awakened him. Crickets chirped and frogs called from the slough. He sat up and felt an overwhelming desire to vomit. The room spun and everything ached.

He blinked in the dim light and tried to discern where he was. Suddenly, Coal Oil Johnny pulled back the blanket that served as a door and walked in.

"Johnny?" Hick said in confusion.

The old man smiled his toothless grin. "You gonna be okay, Sheriff. Won't be sending for the sin eater today."

Hick felt a laugh growing inside him. It came out in a raspy gasp that made him cough. "No, not today," he agreed.

Johnny handed Hick a canteen. "How you come to be in such a spot, Sheriff?"

Hick took the canteen, his hands still handcuffed. He glanced at the old man as he took a long drink. Finally, he replied. "I found the eephus."

Hick's car had been driven to the far side of the Cypress swamp, a lonely place inhabited by snakes and wild animals and little else. Judging by the sun, Hick figured it was close to seven o'clock. It was still daylight, the Fourth of July celebration would not begin until nine o'clock, but Hick knew everyone was already in town. Claire had the perfect opportunity to silence Hick, and would have succeeded if not for Johnny.

Hick poured the water from the canteen over his head and wiped some of the soot from his face. "I gotta get to town quick, Johnny. Is there a car or anyone nearby?"

Johnny shook his head. "You can take Patsy."

Patsy was Johnny's mule, legendary for her stubbornness.

"Will she let me ride her?"

"Let me have a word with her first."

Hick rose unsteadily and followed Johnny outside. He paused, holding onto the door frame as Johnny went to the barn. The shack was on the waterfront, lonely and tiny, barely habitable and exactly as he imagined it. Moments later, Johnny appeared leading an old mule by a tether.

"She don't take to no saddle or harness. You gotta grip her mane, but she's gentle."

"Thank you, Johnny," Hick told him, grasping the withered hand in both of his. "Thank you for everything." Then, with Johnny's help, he climbed onto the mule.

By the time Hick made it back to town, it was close to eight o'clock. The sun was red and undulating, hesitating to dip below the horizon, but the familiar songs of the mosquitoes and crickets signaled nighttime would soon arrive.

He lay across the mule's neck and coughed and gasped. The air felt cool and chilly after the heat of the car. The after effects of the chloral hydrate still left him groggy.

He took the back way into town and left the mule tied behind the sheriff's station. Adam's face registered shock when Hick staggered through the door. "Christ, Hick. Sit down. My God, boy, what happened?"

Hick's face was scraped and cut. It was covered with black soot and ash, and he was bruised. He sank into the chair Adam offered, not caring that Wayne Murphy was standing by the bars of the cell, alert, waiting for his explanation.

"I found out who killed the baby," he told Adam in a

raspy voice while Adam fumbled in a cabinet for the keys to the handcuffs.

Adam unlocked them and Hick rubbed his wrists. He took the water Adam offered and wiped the soot from his face.

Adam stood beside him. "Tell me what's happened."

Hick glanced at the cell that held Wayne Murphy, then he rose and went to Adam's desk. He opened Ross Thompson's metal box and looked at the names of the pickers he had been in contact with the year before. There were several pay stubs made out to Bill Stanton. At some point, Iva Lee must have come to the fields with her daddy.

Hick sat at the desk and put his head in his hands while Adam patiently waited. Finally, Hick looked up. "Adam, Ross Thompson was the father of Iva Lee's baby."

Adam slowly sank into a chair, his face grave and pale. He closed his eyes. "How do you know?"

"You ever look at Floyd's fingers?"

Adam shook his head.

"They're the same as the baby's. Floyd's fingers are webbed."

Hick watched as realization swept over Adam. His eyes grew wide and he shook his head. "What the hell could Ross have been thinking?"

"I guess loneliness can drive a man to do things he'd never do otherwise," Hick replied. He paused and finally added, "Iva Lee didn't kill the baby."

Adam stared at Hick and realization lighted his features. He rose and paced the floor. "I've known Ross Thompson all my life. I can't believe he'd kill a child."

"He didn't."

Adam turned, his face puzzled.

"Claire killed the baby, Adam. And she tried to kill me."

Adam walked to the window and stared, evidently trying to make sure he had heard right. Finally, he asked, "Did you just say Claire Thompson tried to kill you?"

"Chloral hydrate," Hick told him. "She gave it to me in my iced tea and she set my car on fire. It's why the baby was so quiet … why no one heard anything. The baby wasn't dead or asleep, she was drugged and couldn't move."

"Shit," Adam said as he continued to pace. "Horse medicine. Everyone has it, we should have thought of that. But why the slough? Why didn't she just bury the baby? It would have never been found."

"Claire can't dig anymore. Arthritis. Remember how hard Jack said the ground is this year? She had no choice."

Adam's face was rigid. "My God, Hick. First-degree murder. She planned on killing that baby all along."

"As soon as she found out Iva Lee was pregnant. Ross wanted to marry her and Claire wouldn't have it. I think on some level he really loved that girl." He hesitated and lowered his voice. "There was an empty soda bottle on the floor of Ross's truck."

"You don't think Claire…."

"I don't know, Adam. We'll never know."

"I … I can't believe it," Adam said and rubbed his chin. "I've known her all my life."

They were silent and Adam finally said, "Son of a bitch. We've got to arrest Claire Thompson."

Hick's face was drawn. He said nothing but nodded in agreement.

Adam rose. "And those boys are out there with her." He groaned. "What are we going to do about those boys?"

Hick shook his head. "I just want to get this over with." He rose unsteadily and grabbed the desk for support.

"I'll get Wash," Adam offered. "We'll be back in an hour and then we'll head over. We can do this quiet-like. Everyone will be at the park."

As soon as Adam was gone, Hick staggered across the street to the diner. "Maggie," he called, his voice barely more than a whisper.

Maggie came out of the kitchen smiling and said, "I wondered what happened to you when you…." Her smile disappeared when she saw him. "Hickory?"

He stumbled into her arms.

21

Hick showered at the station, inhaling the steam, and coughing hard to clear the smoke from his lungs. He let the water wash over him, stinging all the cuts and bruises, scrubbing the black soot and grime from his face and hands. Finally, he switched the water off. He toweled off, grabbed his extra uniform, and put it on.

For the first time in months, he really looked in the mirror. Jake Prescott was right. He was thinner. His ear was swollen, and the cuts and bruises from Claire dragging him were angry and bloody. A sense of finality draped over him, not unpleasant, but absolute. This job was too much for him. It was time to resign. He pinned on his badge and remembered the first time he had put it on. Back then, he had little concern as to whether he lived or died. Now, he thought of Maggie, thought of the baby in Belgium, and the baby in the slough, and for the first time in years, remembered the preciousness of life.

He walked into the main office of the station and tied

his tie. Wayne Murphy was standing by the bars. "Please, Sheriff," he begged, "you gotta let me go with you. This is the biggest story to hit these parts in its history. I got to be there to watch it unfold."

Hick silently tightened the tie and put his hat on.

Wayne looked desperate. "Sheriff, the town has a right to know."

Hick turned to him. "Do they, Wayne? Do they have a right to have everything they ever believed true swept out from under them? You don't know what it's like to live in a world you can't comprehend. Sometimes the truth is more than a body can stand."

"But I swear to you. I won't embellish anything. I'll just report the facts."

"That's what I'm afraid of."

Hick heard Adam's car stop and Adam and Wash entered. Wash was pale, shaken. He said little, but Hick could see it in his eyes, doubt and disbelief, the truth taunting him like a mischievous child.

Wash silently sat down and Adam marched to the back of the station. He threw open the gun case and pulled out three pistols. Wash looked up dully. "You really think we'll need those?"

Adam squinted one eye and peered into the cylinder. He closed it and told Wash, "She killed that baby in cold blood, Wash. Premeditated. She tried to kill Hick. I ain't takin' no chances."

Hick strapped the holster on. He hadn't carried a gun since the war. It felt heavy around his waist, with the weight of life and death in its barrel.

Lastly, Wash put his gun on and shook his head in anger. "Goin' up to arrest Claire Thompson with guns and handcuffs like she was some goddamned criminal."

"She's a murderer, Wash," Adam said in a quiet voice.

Wash sniffed. "I don't believe it. Hick, surely you made a mistake?"

Hick paused and then said, "Wash, I wish to God I had."

The three men turned to leave and Wayne Murphy made one final appeal. "Boys, please. You gotta take me with you. I'm beggin' you."

Hick turned to him. "Wayne, you've been privy to more than you deserve already. Claire Thompson destroyed that baby … don't let her destroy the town, too. I can't stop you from putting this in the paper, but I can keep all the salacious details out. I can, at least, spare those boys that."

Hick closed the door hearing as Murphy shouted, "Wait!" The men locked the door of the station behind them.

The drive to the Thompson house was made in silence, the only sound that of gravel grinding beneath tires. The moonlight bounced off the occasional puddle, its brilliance startling in the darkness. The rays danced in and out of the cotton rows as they sped past them. Hick tilted his head and leaned slightly out of the window in order to breathe in the damp air. He filled his lungs with it.

The fireworks began in town. Hick watched as a bright flurry of sparks tumbled from the black sky. The boom followed. Adam stopped the car down the road and turned the lights out. Claire was never one for celebrations. Even on the

Fourth of July they kept farmer's hours. At nine o'clock, the Thompson household was dark.

"We need to be careful," Adam whispered. "I don't want them boys to know nothing."

The other two men nodded in agreement.

Quietly, they closed the car doors and crossed the yard. Another blast of color lighted the sky, followed by the inevitable explosion. Hick envisioned Jack and Floyd crouched before their bedroom window watching. There was no way they could be asleep.

They climbed the porch steps and Adam knocked quietly. Moments later, the door opened and Claire peered out. She seemed frail in her old-fashioned nightgown and night cap. The bright moonlight made her appear washed out and older, less capable than she seemed in the daylight. She opened the door a little wider and said, "Adam? What's wrong?" She looked at him and then at Wash, and when her eyes landed on Hick, there was a flash of surprise followed by resignation. "Won't you come in?"

They followed her into the house. It was dark, the only sound inside, the ticking of the old grandfather clock that stood in the entryway. She led them to the sitting room, as if this were any other visit, and there was nothing out of the ordinary in receiving visitors in her nightgown.

Instead of sitting, the three men stood, Adam's arms crossed. While he could look stern, Hick was weary; his hands in his pockets, his shoulders slumped. Wash stood motionless, his face clearly betraying the idea that he didn't believe Claire was guilty.

She rubbed an arthritic knuckle and then looked down at it. "I guess I know why you're here," she finally said.

"Why don't you remind us," Adam responded.

She sat down in the rocker and wrung her hands. "I still don't see what all the fuss is about."

"How can you say that, Claire? You took that baby and—" Hick's voice was louder than he meant it to be. Claire quickly held up a hand. She stood up and moved across the room and closed the door to the boys' bedroom.

Returning to her chair, she said, "You have to know, that baby didn't suffer. I wouldn't have let her suffer."

"You let her die," Adam returned.

"Yes," Claire admitted. "What kind of life would she have had? She had a half-wit for a mother, and a mouse for a father. Ross never could pick the right woman. I never wanted him to marry the first one, but he did. I told him from the start she'd be no use to him. Pretty and dainty. What good is a woman like that to a man, I ask you? I knew she'd never survive childbirth. I told him so. How she begged him to bring the doctor…." Claire shook her head in disgust. "Weak and soft."

The three men stood unmoving as she continued, "I knew I'd end up raising those boys. I wasn't about to raise the child of a moron, too."

"Bill and Rose would have taken her," Hick argued.

Claire laughed a bitter laugh. "They would have taken me, too. Ross had no business being around that child, he was too old. Even if her mind worked fine, and we all know it didn't, it would have been wrong. I know what would have happened. Everything I worked so hard for would have been gone."

"So you had to kill the baby?" Adam asked, his voice rising a little.

"I disposed of a problem, plain and simple. No one knew Iva Lee was pregnant, Ross told me that. There would have been no one on earth to mourn for that child but Ross, and I figured he deserved it. I told him so. I told him if he couldn't solve his own problems, I'd solve them for him."

"What happened to Ross?" Hick asked.

"Ross was meek and gutless," Claire replied in disgust. "He reminded me of his father. I watched my husband come home from the fields, every day his hands bleeding. He wanted a large family, plenty of children. After Ross, I bore child after child, puny, sickly … weak. I knew they'd be nothing but trouble." She shook her head. "Mr. Thompson always cried when his babies died, like the world was gonna miss out on something wonderful. He hadn't carried those children for nine months. They were strangers to him. I knew those children, I nurtured them in my womb and then they were born worthless. A little chloral hydrate in the baby bottle and they just went to sleep. Oh, they never suffered … it's the livin' that do that."

Hick felt his legs grow weak as he stared at Claire Thompson. The six little tombstones in the cemetery flashed before his eyes. Pam had once told him their mother sat in her room for two months after his brother died of meningitis. She never even opened the curtains. Did Claire ever mourn the children she murdered?

Silence filled the room, heavy and stifling. It was finally broken by Adam. "Claire, I am placing you under arrest for the murder of Birdie Lee Stanton. You have the right to remain silent. If you—"

Claire interrupted. "Excuse me, please." She was very pale. "I need a glass of water. Can I get anyone anything? No? I'll be right back."

Hick followed her back to the kitchen. She stood before the sink, stooped, her hands grasping it for support. She heard his step. "I know what you must think of me," she said without turning around. Behind her, Hick saw a bright flash in the sky. "I'm really not a devil. I loved my children. I love my grandchildren." She turned to him. "I want you to take the boys, Hick. Once I'm gone they'll have no one on earth to care for them. Jack and Floyd think of you and Adam as family already. I don't reckon I'll be back here any time soon."

"No, ma'am."

The fields were briefly illuminated by the silver sparks. "I wish it wasn't so dark," she said as another boom reverberated through the room. "I'd give anything to see it all one last time. Just to say good-bye."

Hick watched as she raised the glass to her lips and a sudden thought occurred to him. Just before it reached her mouth, he placed his hand over the rim. He glanced at the counter and saw the bottle of chloral hydrate sitting there. His eyes met hers and then he shook his head. "Not like this, Miss Thompson."

She dropped the glass into the sink, splinters of glass

cascading against the white porcelain. Her head drooped.

"Now what happens?" she asked in a small voice.

"You'll go to jail. It'll be in the papers. There'll be a scandal."

"Yes."

"I can't help you. You brought this on yourself."

"Ross brought this on me."

Hick looked into Claire's aged eyes. Did they ever tear when her children drew their last breath? "You brought this on yourself when you decided to end that child's life. Ross was ready to be a man and take responsibility for what he did. You took something away from Rose and Bill Stanton, something that can't ever be replaced."

"But was I really so wrong?"

"Granny?" a voice called from the doorway. Hick and Claire looked over and saw Jack. "What's happening?"

Adam was behind the child, grave and resolute.

Claire's face grew sad. She crossed the room to her grandson and stared at him for a moment as if seeing him for the first time. She reached out her hand and stroked his cheek. "Jack, I'm going away for a while."

The finale of the fireworks show lit the sky as they led Claire to the police car in handcuffs. Hick saw her glance at the bright sparks as they rained down from the sky, their light briefly illuminating her face. For an instant he thought he saw remorse written there. It was a brief, flitting moment and he realized it was only his own wishful thinking.

22

Yellow cypress leaves lay silent on the black water of Jenny Slough. Autumn's chill bit into clumps of long, waving grass and soggy, gray clouds scudded over the now empty cotton fields. Steam rose from the water, ghostly and vaporous, and caressed the skeletal trees that seemed to give notice of their own impending demise. Hick stood in the dim shadows and watched the quickly moving squall line. The sound of a snapping twig drew his attention and he turned to see Jake Prescott trudging toward him.

"I thought I might find you here," the doctor remarked, pulling a cigar from his pocket and biting off the end.

"I just wanted to see it, the way it was, one last time."

The doctor lit his cigar and puffed meditatively. "Hard to believe in a year or two this will all be soybeans."

"A lot of memories."

The doctor nodded. "There's no standing in the way of progress. Matt Pringle will have a lot more land to farm once these trees are cleared out and this swamp is dammed up."

"Progress," Hick echoed, reaching into his shirt pocket and pulling out a pack of cigarettes.

"I thought Maggie didn't like you smoking."

"Just not at the house." He flipped open the lighter and cupped his hand over the flame.

The doctor shook his head. "You tell her that smoking is good for you. Maybe she should try it."

"She can't stand the smell."

"It's the baby," Jake explained. "When she's further along smells won't bother her anymore." After a pause he asked, "What's she say about the election?"

Hick shrugged. "She thinks I should run again. She says this town needs me."

"And what do you say?"

"I reckon I want to hang onto it … for the time being." After a moment he added, "It's funny how things change. You think things will always stay the same but they never do. My grandfather fished here. Wonder what my kids will do with this place gone."

The doctor puffed his cigar. "Your daddy and I spent hours out here. Some of my best memories are coming out with a frying pan, cornmeal, and some onions. We had us some times when we were young." He seemed lost in thought and then added, "Folks say the levee will make flooding a thing of the past. Still, I'm gonna miss this place."

Hick's eyes swept the eerie beauty of the slough. It was as if the landscape held onto the memories created there. He remembered days spent fishing and nights spent making love. He glanced at the Thompson place. The heavy machinery that would remove the timber sat parked beside the quiet house. "I wonder what Miss Thompson would have thought," he ventured. "The place seems eerie now that everyone's gone."

"Selling off was the best thing Adam could have done for those boys. Farming is so unpredictable."

"I know," Hick replied. "But it seemed like giving up their birthright."

"A birthright can be a fearsome thing. Claire Thompson would have held onto that land kicking and screaming. She would have died to keep it."

"She killed to keep it."

"Yes," the doctor agreed. "Claire Thompson had a hard life and it made her a hard woman. Her world was a place where only the strong survive and she couldn't see past the here and now."

"True. But I reckon there might be a little of Claire in all of us."

"It's the ones that ain't figured that out yet that you got to worry about. Take Wayne Murphy. Cocky, arrogant, son of a bitch who thinks the world is black and white. He thought Claire was just a bad seed and if it helps him sleep at night, then so be it. I often think it was a mercy her dying in jail before the trial. It wouldn't do to drag the past out into the light of day. She did wrong and there ain't a soul on earth who can say otherwise. Still, Claire did good, too. She wasn't plain bad. Few are. You got to take the good and the bad and make 'em fit together."

"And you can do that?" Hick asked. "You can make 'em fit?"

"Hick, I've been in every house in this county. Ain't one of 'em without some kind of skeleton in the closet. There's those who sit on the porch and flaunt their demons, and there's those who scurry like rats in the shadows."

Hick considered what the doctor said. "I reckon we're all about the same underneath."

"The truth of the matter ain't always the easiest thing to wrap your arms around. I ain't no better or no worse than the next guy. My own humanness depends on me remembering that. You knowing that makes you a better sheriff."

"Mercy," Hick mumbled to himself.

"What's that?"

"Mercy," Hick repeated. "My dad always said it was what set us apart from animals. The fact that human beings had the capacity for mercy. I used to laugh at him and his patient ways. The kindness he showed to the backward farm boys, or to Coal Oil Johnny. I never understood how an educated man could waste his time with folks like that." He paused and then added, "Funny how much I still learn from him."

"Your daddy was the best man I knew."

"Yes," Hick agreed grinding out his cigarette beneath his foot. He gazed once more at the slough, lost in thought. It was still a place, vast and unpredictable, but its wildness had diminished with time. Soon it would be just another cotton or soybean field. It would be tamed, and its domestication would deny its former mystery. He couldn't know as he stood there that he no longer looked weary. Instead, he had the satisfied expression of one who had fought a hard battle and survived.

The doctor must have noticed this because he said, "You remind me more of your daddy every day."

Hick laughed. "You're forgetting. He was the 'magic man'."

"No," the doctor returned. "I'm not."

Thunder rolled in the distance, faint across the delta.

"Sounds like another storm's coming," Jake remarked.

Hick turned to go. "There's always another storm."

Acknowledgments

The publication of this book is a dream come true and it could not have happened without the help and support of so many people. Thank you to those friends who believed in me and encouraged me to not give up ... you know who you are. I am greatly indebted to my readers and critiquers: Russell, Paula, Tom, Sharon, Bob, and Katherine. And I am most assuredly grateful to Kristina Blank Makansi and Brad R. Cook for believing in this story. Lastly, thank you to my family for not begrudging the hours spent in the Virginia Woolf suite of our basement.

About the Author

As a child, Cynthia A. Graham spent every weekend and vacation in the cotton belt of Missouri where she grew to love the mystery and beauty of the stark, delta plane. Today, Cynthia lives in St. Louis where she graduated Summa Cum Laude from the University of Missouri – St. Louis with a B.A. in English. She has won several awards for her short stories and has been published in both university and national literary publications. She is a member of the Historical Novel Society and the St. Louis Writer's Guild.

Beneath Still Waters is her first novel.

CPSIA information can be obtained at www.ICGtesting.com
Printed in the USA
LVOW09s0351300515

440389LV00001B/1/P